AN AFFAIR ABROAD

The Love Story of Nadia & Maximus

−2y

T.K. RICHARDS

T.K. Richards

EXCLUSIVE

This is the beginning of Nadia & Maximus's story. To learn more about these characters and receive bonus content, including a **bonus chapter, Second Honeymoon**, exclusive to my email subscribers. Sign up for my newsletter here:

https://tkrichardsnewsletter.ck.page
www.tkrichards.com

First printing, 2021

LNK Publishing

ISBN-13: 978-1-7370438-0-5

www.tkrichards.com

To the single ladies.
May you find love.

CHAPTER I

NADIA

'This is humbling. Sitting in a room full of strangers because I can't get over a man. What a bunch of losers. Wait a minute, I'm here so I guess I'm a loser, too. Why would I take advice from Carmen 'Can't Keep a Man' Woods? I would die if any of my friends saw me in here. Note to self— Give Carmen a tongue-lashing tomorrow— better yet, never mention I was here.

I can barely hear myself think with Lady Chatterley sitting next to me. For the love of God, someone please shut this woman's mouth. I have been smiling and nodding the entire time she has been yapping her purple lips, but I haven't heard a word she's said.

Well what do we have here? This one seems pretty full of herself. I can tell from looking at her designer shoes whatever problem she's facing, it is most likely her fault. I shouldn't say such things. I don't know this woman, yet still I want to call her Ms. Look at Me. She can't stop looking in the mirror long enough to see what is actually happening in the world—like how I am intensely watching and judging her. Shame on me. A giant panther could have entered the room and she wouldn't know it. Look up sweetie you're not cute enough to be clueless.

My God! Who let King Kong out of her cage? Note to self, 'don't let her kick me in the ass.' She has to be the tallest, most statuesque white woman I have ever seen. Please don't sit by me, please don't sit by me. Whew! That was a close one. I might slip and say something slick and she would wipe the floor with me. Next mental note— Nadia, stop talking about these people.

Now what do we have here? Possible lesbians, perhaps? Jeez, I hope not. I can't bear to hear what issues they are having. I thought once you gave up on men, you should be happy by process of elimination. Right? How could any woman on woman relationship have problems when a man isn't involved? Guess I'll find out soon enough. If they do turn out to be a couple, I'll treat myself with donuts tonight. I beg someone, anyone, gas me now.

Is the therapist here already? Is she one of these women I have talked about horribly, waiting for the right time to speak? I don't want to be the guinea pig, nor do I want to sit here and waste my time looking at strangers all night. I have talked about them to myself which I really need to work on. Note to self— Work on your bullshit, and stop talking about people.'

The metal door creaks as it flies open from the hands of a petite, well-dressed woman, rushing in with folders pressed against her chest. Her maroon- colored lipstick, and black cat-eye frames announced she was fashionable, and perhaps well paid, which was a good sign.

As her heels clanked across the wooden floor, I had a change of heart. This didn't seem like a place I belonged. As she continued to get settled in, I stood and grabbed my sweater from the back of my seat. Avoiding eye contact with everyone, I fixed my mouth to say, 'I'm so sorry, but I can't stay,' but was intercepted by the therapist.

Coherently and unapologetically she spoke. "Forgive me for running late, I couldn't get my husband off of me."

'Wait, what? Did the therapist greet us with personal information? About herself? Maybe I will stay after all.'

I repositioned my sweater and made myself comfortable, eager to hear what she was going to say next.

"Allow me to start by asking you all this question. Are you open to sharing your deepest, darkest, most liberating sexual encounters with the people you see in this room?"

The room fell silent. We all looked around at each other with skepticism. Crickets chirping outside the windows, music from cars passing by, and chatter from the hallways filled the room as our whispers remained on pause.

"I urge you to answer my question honestly, as it is important for you to be successful in this class. My name is Dr. Bartley, and I'm here to help you— help yourself."

She looked around the room, assessing us from what I could gather. No one had found their voice to answer her question, and as the silence continued, she began writing in her notebook, looking up at us from the rim of her glasses.

"I'm going to assume those who have remained seated are responding yes. Yes? Okay then. Let's get started. You with the mirror." She pointed to the girl I nicknamed Ms. Look at Me.

"Me?" she asked, tapping her designer shoes.

Her heavy lined eyes looked confused, and her caramel face had a bit of fear written on it suddenly.

"Yes, you. You are primping in the middle of the day. Why?" Dr. Bartley questioned.

"Don't you want to know my name first?"

"We'll get to names a little later. Right now, I'm interested in knowing why you are staring at yourself in the middle of the day? In a class for people who are sexually frustrated no less."

"Um, because you never know who you're going to meet," replied mirror girl.

"Did you plan on meeting someone to impress in here?" Dr. Bartley asked.

"Maybe."

"And how about you?" Dr. Bartley pointed her pen towards me.

"What about me?" I asked looking her in the eye, past the glass on her ebony frames.

"I saw you getting ready to leave as I walked in. Tell me why?"

"I had second thoughts about staying," I firmly replied, refusing to allow her to bully me into submission like the first two women.

"May I ask why?"

"I don't think I belong in here." I sassed.

"So why did you sit back down?"

"Honestly, when you blurted out you couldn't get your husband off of you, I was intrigued. That was one hell of a way to enter a room," I said, causing a stir.

"Your response tells me you are interested in other people's lives. Am I right?"

"I, I, I wouldn't use those exact words. I just found what you said to be very honest. You know. I have never met a person bold enough, or unafraid to enter a room as their true self. Nowadays, everyone is either faking it, or trying to be something they're not." I explained with surprising support from the room.

The girl I labeled as Lady Chatterley sat opposite of me, humming in agreeance, catching the attention of Dr. Bartley.

"You appear to have something to add." The good doctor looked down her nose. "What brings you here?"

"A former attendee recommended I sit in one of your sessions." She stammered.

"Do you often take advice from unlicensed professionals?"

"I beg your pardon." Lady Chatterley scoffed.

"What I am asking you is, where is your own mind? Your own train of thought? Where is your courage to do what you think you should be doing? Don't worry. We'll work on those factors in the weeks to come."

I read the room. Of seven attendees, three sat in their seats with expressions of enthusiasm on their faces. The possible couple were having a conversation with their eyes, and Lady Chatterley appeared to be uneasy as she raised her hand to speak like we were in school.

"Can you start with someone else? Please? I don't want to go first."

Dr. Bartley answered with an impish grin across her lips. "Of course. Class let me inform you. I am all about expressing how one truly feels. I encourage my class to speak freely and honestly. I will push you to stop hiding and reveal the person you are when no one else is around. Your true self. You will have to get personal, and dirty, and detailed in here, so again I ask, is everyone in here comfortable with my methods? And this time I would like a verbal yes or no."

"Yes." Everyone answered except me.

"I was right earlier. I don't belong here. Good luck to you all," I said, avoiding direct eye contact with the room.

The immediate silence was uncomfortable. Quickly, I crossed my tote with my sweater and jetted to the exit. Lately, I have been second guessing myself about everything. I know to follow my gut, yet I disobeyed it, and sat back down. *'Big mistake.'*

Trust is one of the areas I needed extreme help with, and trusting a room full of strangers with my most personal, intimate details is not where I wanted to begin that journey. Such a conversation could be had with my closest friends, whom I'd be spending the day with tomorrow. *'I won't tell them about the class. Only about dumping Evan. They already call me Naïve Nadia. No need to make it worse.'*

Despite the overcast and heavy weekend traffic, I wiggled my way through the backroads of Charlotte to Taylor's shower. Five minutes late, but on time before the bride threw a hissy fit, I arrived with the cheese and fruit tray, bottles of chardonnay, and tequila. The shower was a hit, filling the country club with the bride and groom's side of the family, an overflowing table of gifts, and libations flowing amongst the room.

The party was near its end when Levi, the groom, arrived to pick up the gifts, and his bride to be. He tried to break up the party and tear Taylor away from us, until it became clear we weren't ending our night early.

Outnumbered and aware of the company before him, he loaded his car with the presents, and waved his scrawny arms at us as he left.

We snacked on the remaining food trays, to balance the number of bottles we were most likely to empty. Our group never needed to go to a party. We were the party.

Shannon, the outspoken wild one, was in rare form. Always forward and unapologetically direct. Tonight, was no different. After over indulging on tequila, she overstepped with invasive questions for the bride. "Are you ever going to tell us what he is like in bed?"

The room chuckled as Isla passed the near empty bottle of tequila around the table.

Taylor smirked. "You never share such information about the one."

Shannon's face stiffened. Her golden eyes locked on Taylor, and her lips barely hid the cracked smile she forced. "He's that good huh."

All of us squealed in high pitches followed by laughter, while Taylor blushed, revealing the unspoken details, simply by smiling so hard. Her rosy flushed cheeks could no longer hold her resting bitch face.

"Good for you Taylor," I said. "You are right. It's none of our business."

"What's going on with you and Evan?" Taylor questioned as her caramel hands reached for the last drop of tequila.

"Not a damn thing. I know you guys think he is a keeper, and he does look great on paper, but **I** am just not into him." I emphasized.

"Why not? I wish a man like Evan would sweep me off of my feet." Isla scowled in my direction.

"Look, I already feel bad about stringing him along. Trust me on this one. If you knew why I have to break up with him, you might sympathize with me."

With great hope, I wanted them to take me at my word. Such a wish might have been possible if they were of sober mind. "Then tell us why," they said in unison, like a rehearsed choir.

I finished off the remaining tequila in my glass, and chased it with a squeeze of lime between my teeth. Gasping from the burning pains in my chest, I bought myself a few moments before sharing my quandary. "He is incapable of giving me an orgasm." I hid my face with shame, peeping at my friends through the cracks of my fingers.

Taylor and Isla looked at each with smirks between them, Khai took a sip from her cup with raised eyebrows, and Shannon couldn't help but be Shannon.

"Come again? No pun intended." Shannon chuckled.

I knew her too well to know her pun was indeed intended. Once the banter and laughter faded, I pled my case.

"I've never had an orgasm with him. Sex with him is so horrible, I can't describe it," I blurted, hiding my face.

My friends looked at each other in silence, which is strange because they always have something to say. I could tell from looking at each one of them, they were calculating their responses, and waiting each other out to speak first.

"You are going to let a good man go, because of bad sex. You're crazy, Nadia. Do you know the percentage of women who have to fake it in the sack, but have a good man to come home to? Do you think a lot of women are sexually satisfied? Let me break it down for you. Studies show only twenty percent of people, married or single, actually experience the best sex of their lives. Get you a vibrator, handle your business, and keep your man." Shannon lectured looking down at me from her ginger colored nose.

"You seem to have it all figured out don't you, Sha? Pass the wine please?" I asked Khai in desperate need of a swig to survive Shannon's sermon.

"You know I'm the one in this circle who knows the most about sex." Shannon bragged.

"Just because your yellow ass talks about it the most, doesn't mean you know the most." Isla added.

"And you do? As I was saying, you better not throw a perfectly good man to the woods when the rest of us are meeting pathological liars, cheaters, sword fighters, video game freaks, and what not." Shannon definitively rested her case.

After taking a bow, she tooted her own horn further, telling me her advice was free of charge *this time*. I balled up a paper napkin from the table and threw it at her.

Khai then decided to chime in. "Have you told him he was bad in bed?"

I admitted I didn't want to hurt his feelings. And with that statement, I proved to be a walking nincompoop.

Men rarely make decisions with the consideration of a woman's feelings. They live their lives selfish and entitled with the world handed to them, while women have historically made the dumbest decisions in their life based on a man. Girls choose a college based on a boy. The television show Felicity was surely about a million girls worldwide. Women have agreed to public marriage proposals, to save the integrity of a man she has no intention of being with long term.

Always the nurturer, women everywhere are sparing a man's feelings. Ignoring their own needs and wants and desires, to be pleasing to or for a man. I know this firsthand.

The love of my life, Dylan, or who I thought was the love of my life, wasted my early twenties. I could have moved to New York and become a dancer, or experienced the rough streets of NYC and become a groomed writer at a major publication.

Instead, I met a big shouldered sexual God with a head full of course hair, and a smile that could charm the panties off of a nun. It is because of him, I stayed in North Carolina after college. Afraid if I left he would find someone better, or we would grow apart, or he wouldn't want me anymore, and cheat on me because of the distance.

It is also because of him, I have yet to trust a man with my heart, and overanalyze everything in my relationships. His ghost lives in my head and my bedroom, even though he did turn out to be a serial cheater, with me living in the same city as him, a compulsive liar, and extraordinary gas lighter.

Evan is better than Dylan in every way, except between the sheets. His kindness is appreciated, he calls often, is a considerate human being, and his resume is desirable. But that's it.

My friends couldn't understand the torture I feel when we're intimate. He's too good of a person to tell the brutal truth. My only solution was to end the relationship, and leave the hurtful comments to his next partner.

"Nadia, Evan is crazy about you. Shannon is right. Fake it and stroke his ego, then get yours with a toy when you need it." Khai encouraged, raising her sketched eyebrows as she took another sip.

'I don't think she bought what she said either.'

The mention of a bedroom toy, served as a segue for Shannon to become livelier. Describing what brand she recommends. Exaggerating with tales of how she became addicted to one in particular.

Unfortunately, Shannon's wild stories didn't remove the attention from me completely. "Do you love him? Like at least a little bit?" Taylor asked.

"I have love for him, but no, I can't say I love him, love him."

"You guys, this is about Dylan again." Taylor teased me. "Look at her. She is still hung up on the douchebag with the bomb-diggety dick."

"This is not about him." I lied.

"Yes, it is! You are still hung up on your old flame who cheated on you, and made you feel insecure about yourself. All because the sex was *immaculate* as you put it?"

"This is not about him for the last time."

I convinced no one, but I refused to let on. Beneath the digs and jabs, I knew my friends were concerned about my well-being. When I love, I love hard. And getting over Dylan was beyond rough in the beginning.

I suffered extreme dark days during that time, and I knew my circle never wanted to see me in such a state again.

"We want you to be happy," said Isla. "Forget about that

lame prick, and move on with your life. It's been what three years?"

"Five," I mumbled.

Taylor could tell from the sour look I gave her, I was pissed she brought Dylan up. She sat quietly, while everyone else piled on with their thoughts about what I should do.

Casually she interrupted. "I think breaking up with Evan was the right thing to do. If a guy isn't satisfying you in the bedroom, you will not take him seriously. I know I wouldn't. And look at you. Stunning and miserable. If he doesn't make you happy after doing all the things you ask of him, then he isn't the one. You want magic. And fire. And passion. I get it."

"Well you just answered my questions about your sex life." Shannon clinked her glass with Khai.

Taylor scolded Shannon for prying yet again, while I fought the urge to remain upset with the one person now showing me support. I was missing everything she mentioned. I was bored and unhappy with Evan. I wanted what I had with Dylan, before his true colors were revealed, and what she had with Levi.

Dylan's whip appeal kept me thinking about him all of the time. My phone was glued to my hand, making sure I didn't miss his call. I yearned for his touch in the middle of the day. Snuck home during lunch for quickies. Everything Taylor said was true. When a man isn't doing his job in the bedroom, he doesn't cross your mind, or give you the shivers when you least expect it. I never looked for Evan's call, or yearned for his touch. I tolerated him because he was nice, and I suffered from the responsibility to be polite. To be a kind woman.

Sex shouldn't be a deal breaker, but it was a deal breaker. After nearly six months, I had given my best to a dreamy guy, waiting for something to kick in.

Shannon joked. "Dylan really dicmatized you."

She was correct. I have been comparing every man I date to him. At some point, I joined the club of women who had a hard time getting over a man not worth my tears, time, and energy. The worst men always handled their business in the sack, and are the hardest to move on from.

Old women speak truth when they say, you have to lie under a new one to get over an old one, but that statement needs some amending. You have to lie under a better one in my opinion.

"Let us set you up with someone," Khai suggested.

"I'm not donating my reserve dick," said Shannon.

"Wait, what?" I asked. "I don't want any of your hand me downs. I can find a man on my own thank you."

"It's not about finding a man. It's about getting you laid with some good *D* so you can move on with your life. I knew a guy so hung he gave me a bladder infection. You might be able to handle him. I sure couldn't." Khai snickered.

"Thanks, but no thanks to the Emergency Room dick. I'll pass."

We burst with laughter. Isla stood at the table and made a toast to finding me a thoroughbred in the sack. They all raised their glasses. "To finding Nadia a thoroughbred in the sack!"

Glasses clinked amongst them, as I held my head low in humiliation. Taylor diverted the attention back to her with news about our upcoming seven-day wedding getaway. She discussed the details and itinerary of our trip to London in a week.

Khai lit up at the mention of the word's getaway and week, expressing she was overdue for a break, and in desperate need of some girl time.

Taylor made the trip sound surreal, constantly repeating, "We are going to live like The Royals, or at least close to it. Levi has rented buses, and a private chauffeur during our stay, along with scoring us access to clubs, and passes for a major festival happening on the weekend."

Taylor made it sound as if we were going to party like rock stars, which was up her alley. She devoted the past year to plan her extravagant affair: scheduled family activities to occupy us during the week, designated days for rest— which we were going to need after wine tasting, game day, and a two-hour train ride to Paris.

I had been eyeing flights to Ibiza, Spain from London, and asked if any time would be permitted to do something of our own choosing. "I want to see the big magnetic rock, Es Vedra. It's supposed to have healing powers."

Taylor shut down the notion of us not obeying her every command, for her wedding, and quickly dismissed my query. "We have a jam-packed week. Maybe next time." She continued with her speech, killing the mood, and our buzz with the nonstop details.

Finally, Shannon saved us with her usual antics. She interrupted Taylor and asked, "Are we going shopping, and what kind of men do they have to offer over there?"

Isla was now tipsy slurring in her words, and added. "I heard a rumor the men in London are the world's worst lovers."

"I guess we'll find out won't we Isla." Shannon gave Isla a high-five.

Their shenanigans returned the liveliness back into the room, and we sipped a few more rounds, listening to Isla and Shannon match each other wit for wit. An oldie but goodie came on the radio, and we sang along and grooved in the open area by the table, dancing our drunken heads to the tunes, until Levi returned to shuttle us home.

CHAPTER 2
LONDON

Visiting a different continent, and country, could now be checked off my bucket list. The anticipated destination wedding weekend was upon us, and thanks to Khai upgrading my seats to first class, the long flight went smoothly.

By early evening, all of the bridal party assembled in Taylor's suite, to check in and receive our orders. Wired with excitement, even though we were on a tightly run ship, we tended to the list of duties given to us.

While welcoming the guests at the reception in the hotel lounge, the girls and I scoped the premise for possible prospects. Levi's family provided certifiable eye candy, as well as a few of the hotel staff.

The start to our getaway seemed promising. After exchanging pleasantries with both families, Isla took it upon herself to ask the concierge of the Friday night happenings.

According to the itinerary, we were scheduled to go clubbing Sunday night, but we were too excited to spend our first night in Europe stuck at the hotel. Secretly huddled in the lobby, Isla whipped out a list of events to check out nearby. It was settled. We were going out on the town. Now, we had to break it to Taylor.

She wasn't thrilled with our plan, especially since she was unable to join us. Veering from her itinerary, wasn't how she imagined the start of the weekend, but she graciously gave us access to the limousine for the night.

After a quick change into skimpy outfits, the fab five minus 1 made its first stop. A few blocks away from the hotel, a nearby pub stood on the corner. The girls and I looked at each other confused. Surely, the concierge didn't think we would have a good time, at a place playing music we didn't know how to label. The place was practically empty, and the scene was trite.

Without mumbling a sound between us, we backtracked back into the limo, fearing the night was going to be a bust.

Isla asked the driver, Tony, if he was familiar with any of the places on the concierge's list. He scoffed multiple times as his eyes read from top to bottom. He then asked if she wanted to hear the truth. Isla nodded yes.

With confidence he said, "You ladies won't enjoy any of the places on this list. These are the safe tourist attractions. A group of young ladies like yourself would enjoy the clubs the locals go to."

We pretended to have a private sidebar conversation about what we should do, but Tony could hear us.

"I say we stick to the list. I'm not trying to be a human trafficking victim," said Khai.

"Who would buy and sell you Khai." Isla snickered.

Khai nudged her then added. "We are not home. We can't trust anyone. Not even Tony here, no offense." She motioned her head towards him.

"Taylor said he is bonded and will be with us all week, so I'm guessing we can trust him." Shannon raised a brow.

Khai asked Tony a serious round of questions, typed out his full name and license number in an email to her sister, and made him swear he would do as we commanded.

"I will take good care of your party. Would it be of interest to you, if I drove by the hot spots not mentioned on the list?" Tony asked.

The four of us agreed with a simple nod.

"And Tony sir, I am live streaming this outing, so our whereabouts will be public," Khai announced.

"Sounds good Madame."

The line in the car rang loudly enough for us to hear in the rear. Tony called a friend by the name of Prano, who had connections with nighttime entertainment. He explained our dilemma to the high-pitched voice on the line. We struggled to understand what was being said between them, due to their heavy accents and broken British lingo, which sounded alike yet different somehow.

The background of his whereabouts sounded like the place we needed to be. We gave him the okay and arrived at Tower Nightclub, placed in the middle of a block, with a heavy line of people waiting behind a velvet rope.

Tony drove us directly in front of the entrance, and thanks to his contact, we bypassed the line to go inside. "No woman left behind." Khai reminded us as we entered.

The place was leveled with people of all colors, and the music was blasting techno rave tunes. The music scene was different than in the States. The hot songs were blends, mixed over a faster house music sound, which was popular in the U.K, thumping with heavy bass lines and noisy effects.

We settled at our table sharing appetizers and cocktails, when the music transitioned to classic reggae dancehall, my favorite genre. Off I went to the middle of the dancefloor to show off my moves.

I had to create my own space on the floor. Once I let loose, the crowd surrounded me as I threw my cilantro colored fringe dress and hair around.

Heavy into the moment, and feeling alive for the first time in a while, I danced as if I knew a crowd was watching. A spotlight appeared above me, singling me out in front of everyone.

The crowd surrounding me clapped and cheered me on, fueling my ego to carry on the way I did at frat parties back in college. I fed into the way they were receiving me— until another dancer came from the darkness, and made his way into my light.

He circled me before engaging, and when the beat dropped he began thrusting and winding on me from the rear. I felt his bulge against my back, so I turned to get a good look at him. He wasn't the most attractive man, nor was he my type, but I couldn't deny he had rhythm.

I paused and watched him with my hands placed up on my hips, doing moves I couldn't dream of in an acrobatic fashion. He taunted me to battle him, and instead of gracefully giving him his respect, I waited for his moment to end, then joined him once the bass kicked. I circled him, throwing my flimsy strands everywhere, and challenged him as if he were an old companion.

He responded to my invitation as if we knew one another, and went back and forth creating a frenzy in the crowd. I let him get the best of me until it was quitting time, then I surprised him with a slowly risen high kick, and held it in place for a few seconds.

While holding my balance, I tossed my hair and pretended to file my nails, causing the crowd to go wild. My consort bowed down to me, and I in return curtsied him. Together we bowed to the crowd as they applauded us, then shook hands followed by a friendly hug, whispering compliments to one another.

I strutted back to my table for some much-needed rest, but before I could sit, I was asked to join Isla in the ladies' room. We snaked our way through the crowd when I noticed a short, latte colored guy appeared to be following us. I freshened up in the mirror while Isla used the loo, debating if I wanted to worry her about the suspicious man.

Upon our exit, the guy in question stood with his back against the wall near the men's pisser. I grew nervous.

He stepped forward. "Pardon me, I'm friends with Tony, the chauffeur who brought you here. Hayden's my name but people call me Prano."

Immediately I recognized the high-pitched tone. "Nice to meet you Prano. I'm Nadia, and this is Isla."

I imagined him as a tall, slim, fair-skinned figure from his voice on the phone. He didn't match the person I created in my head at all, but he was still cute enough. His eyes bounced between Isla and I, and he smiled on the side of his mouth. He was just as nervous to meet us as we were him.

"Thanks for letting us come in tonight," said Isla.

"It was no problem at all. Really. Lovely meeting you both. I planned on coming over to your table and introducing myself, and a few of my associates here tonight. But before I could do so, the Deejay wanted me to find you." Prano pointed at me. "He wants to thank you personally for putting on a show out there. You have some really nice moves."

I blushed like an idiot. My cheeks were so full, they nearly burst. It was as if I had never received a compliment before. "Thank you. If he really sent you out of your way, I guess we can go say hi." I looked to Isla for confirmation it was okay with her.

"If you wouldn't mind following me, I'll take you to the stage." Prano led with a step.

"I guess it's okay." Isla shrugged her shoulders. "If he is fine, I call dibs."

'Dibs on a man.'

"Isla, please. I'm not going there with you tonight. Besides, he asked to meet me."

The side of the stage was guarded by a hefty security team, sectioned off by a velvet rope. Limited seating was available, so we stood and waited, too long for Isla's taste.

Song after song blasted from the nearby speakers, still no sign of this deejay who wanted to show his gratitude. Isla grew impatient and asked Prano to escort us back to our table, without asking if I was ready to bail.

"You go ahead. I'll be right behind you," I said.

Her face grimaced. "We travel in pairs. Always."

I convinced her to give the guy a few more minutes, as a line dance song came on. Prano assured us his friend would join us in a few minutes, claiming to know the playlist.

Rudely, Isla suggested. "Can you light a fire under him."

Prano climbed the stairs to the dimly lit booth, signaling thumbs up from above. Moments later, the music changed and Prano returned with an average height, slightly tanned white boy behind him. He was medium-build, with curly brown hair cut low on the sides and nape of his neck, thick eyebrows, hooded light brown eyes, and a square jaw outlined from a five o'clock shadow. A crisp white fitted t-shirt hugged his chest, and tailored white jeans hung correctly around his waist. It was hard to not stare at him.

"Ladies this is Mash. Mash this is Nadia, the lady you asked to meet, and her friend Isla," said Prano, smiling at Isla.

"Nice to meet you ladies, especially you, the dancing queen." He kissed the back of my hand.

I blushed. Unable to speak as the gorgeous specimen eyed me from head to toe. When the cat finally let go of my tongue, I flirtatiously said to him, "Dancing Queen. Stop. I was just enjoying the music."

"Ah, an American. You surprise me yet again."

"I know we don't sound sophisticated like you Brits. You're easy to understand by the way. I was having trouble earlier with your friend."

"I love your accent." He gazed into my eyes without blinking.

I blushed again, looking at his full lips, then his eyes, then his lips once more. *'They look tasty,'* I thought to myself, searching for the right words to say next.

My accent was all over the place at times. I had my home voice, which was country twang, my work voice, which was considered proper, and my Geechee tongue, which I spoke with my grandmother. Sometimes I spoke all three without realizing it.

Finally, I complimented him in return. "I love yours as well."

"Tonight, must be my lucky night. A great beauty gave me the boost I needed to get through this set. You see I just arrived back in town for a big event tomorrow, and I'm fatigued to say the least," he confessed.

"When Prano said your name, I thought I recognized it. We're here for a destination wedding, and there is a big outdoor party we're going to tomorrow. I remember reading your name on the flyer."

"Yeah, a few hours away in Glastonbury. I won't rest until my set is over. As soon as I'm done here I'll load up again, and hit the road. When is the wedding?" he asked, looking at his watch.

I felt I had bored him quickly, and didn't want to humiliate myself further. "Next Sunday. Well, good luck tomorrow. It was nice meeting you," I said, salvaging my pride before being dismissed.

"My apologies. I checked my watch to see how long I have before this song ends." He explained.

"I understand. I don't want to keep you from working. We need to get going anyway, since we have an early morning."

"So, you're here for a week?" He grinned.

I nodded yes.

"I hope this isn't too forward, but if I give you my information, will you reach out to me. I'd really like to talk with you some more, maybe you could stop by my tent tomorrow. Check out my set? If it's cool with you?"

"I'd love to."

"Here's my card. All of my social media is listed, and this is my mobile on the back. I really hope I hear from you Nadia."

I studied the card, thinking of the perfect response before walking away. *'Talk to you soon. See you later. I'll be sure to call.'*

"You will," I replied, lifting my head from studying his information.

Our lips met surprisingly. *'Mmm. An accidental kiss. Or was it. He didn't pull away so easy.'*

We shared a smile from our faux pas moment, and for a few seconds locked eyes, until he recognized the song was about to end.

"I was aiming for your forehead but you— I should apologize, but I'm not sorry." He admitted.

"It's fine. Don't miss your cue. I'll be in touch." I sauntered away slowly.

He winked his left eye at me, then ran up the stairs to the booth, while Prano led Isla and I through the crowd.

I'm not sure if I walked, glided, or floated to our table, but I was in heaven, as well as in shock. This was the first time I found a Caucasian man attractive, and felt chemistry so powerful with a stranger at first sight.

Men of different persuasions made passes at me before, but I never flirted back. Never gave them a chance, or a second look. But this time I engaged. A smoldering, brown-eyed babe, with skin the color of buttermilk had my stomach doing pirouettes. And I liked it.

Before taking a seat, I slipped my cell number to Prano, and asked him to give it to Mash. As my head was in the clouds, I could hear Isla telling the girls about our thirty-minute disappearance.

I was in a zone, off somewhere with my thoughts, fascinating about my encounter. The kiss. The feel of his lips. The way his eyes shone. The way I wanted to ditch my friends, force my way back into VIP, and taste him once more.

Moments later Shannon shoved me, waking me from my trance. They were all staring at me, waiting for me to chime in and validate Isla's rambling. I had a lot to say, yet speechless at the same time. I sat there smiling at them like those masks you see at Mardi Gras, dodging their questions, and staring past them at the tinted glass on the booth.

I wondered if he was heavy into his job, or looking at me, too. "Earth to Nadia. Tony is waiting for us at the door." Shannon nudged me to rise as I took one last look at the stage.

I was hounded on the way back to the hotel. The girls begged me for details, but I wasn't ready to discuss it. What was there to discuss? A gorgeous man asked to meet me, accidentally kissed me, and gave me his number. I was still processing it all myself— My intrigue and arousal of the man.

Honestly, I didn't know how to communicate what I was feeling or thinking, and lucky for me Khai was too tired to badger me once we made it to our room. Before falling asleep

23

she playfully said, "Don't think you are off the hook. I want answers in the morning." Then dozed off within seconds.

Lying across my bed, I giggled and smiled to myself like a simpleton. I needed to shower the club scent off of my skin, but couldn't pull myself out of my daydream to do so. Sleep was calling me, but my thoughts were on repeat of the accidental kiss that moved me, and then my phone buzzed.

Prano delivered and gave Mash my number. He texted.

M: *I'd like to see you before I get on the road.*
Can I stop by?

I didn't want to say yes and seem desperate. I also didn't want to say no. I wanted to see him as well. I was nervous to talk to him in a quiet setting with just the two of us at such a late hour, so I hesitated for a long time not knowing how to respond. The next message popped up.

M: *I hope I didn't wake you.*

I held the phone close to my chest, while my mind raced on how to reply. I was in London, on a destination wedding vacation with love in the air, and a new experience on my heels.

Filled with uncertainty and giddiness, I decided I would take full advantage of whatever came my way, live outside of my comfort zone and replied.

N: *The Mandarin in Hyde Park.*

I took the shortest shower of my life, and threw on a pair of jeans and a fitted tee, washed off my make-up, brushed my teeth, and moisturized my face so he could see me in my natural state. I applied some lip balm in case our lips touched again, and pulled my hair back into a ponytail as the next message came through.

M: *I'm in the lobby.*

As the elevator doors closed I became uneasy. '*I should have made him wait to see me,*' I thought, but it was too late. I was already on the ground floor, and there he was, standing near the front desk waiting for me.

I walked over to his leering face, exuded with confidence, and plopped in front of him. Twisting and turning about flirtatiously, as the bass in his voice nearly made my knees buckle.

"My crew is out front giving me hell for coming over here." He grinned with his head down. "I couldn't stop talking about you. Even if it's only for a few minutes, I had to see your face."

"I'm flattered." My cheeks flushed.

A short silence occurred while we stared at each other, smiling in between eye contact, waiting for the other to speak.

"I must admit you make me nervous. Do I make you, nervous?" he asked, in a deep tone.

"A little."

"That must mean something. I hope we find out what." He seduced me with a tempting look in his eyes.

"Yeah, I hope so, too."

"Forgive me for staring. I'm normally cool. It's something about you...I can't take my eyes off of you."

"You know you didn't have to come all the way over here. I could have sent you a picture."

"It wouldn't have been the same."

"Why not?" I tilted my head.

"Because I can't kiss a picture," he said, then stole my lips.

He pecked them delicately, once with his eyes open looking into mine. I returned the gesture and closed my eyes, tasting a trace of liquor that mixed well with the sweetness of his tongue as we locked lips.

We lingered, long enough to hold hands, and make our first official kiss perfect. And it was, perfection from two strangers.

"That was exactly how I imagined it." His eyes held mine.

I unlocked my hands from around his. Our index fingers remained intertwined.

"I'm glad you came to see me." I felt my heart skip a beat.

"So am I. I know what I'll be dreaming about on the bus. I'll tell you about it tomorrow," he said, letting go of my fingers as he backed away to the sound of the horn blowing for him outside.

"I look forward to it. Good night." I walked backwards towards the elevator.

He waved, high-stepping to the exit. "I've changed my mind. Send me a picture!" He shouted across the empty lobby, captivating me with his perfectly lined teeth until the steel doors closed between us.

CHAPTER 3
MAXIMUS

En route to the festival, every corner of the bus had something different going. Some slept, read, or sat quietly to themselves, while others made the drive entertaining. Telling jokes, playing card games, passing bottles of hooch, and making bets of sporting events back home.

The sweetest of dreams filled my head as I napped, and when I woke I admired the country roadside of the terrain.

At times, I caught a glimpse of myself in the reflection of the window, grinning about my late-night visit, and planning what to say when I saw him. Three hours later, we arrived in Glastonbury. The butterflies returned to my stomach, fluttering in circles, and my chested tightened in knots. The feeling was familiar, yet scary. I hadn't felt those flutters in years, and to feel them so quickly about a man I knew nothing about, threw me for a loop.

The field was packed with free-spirited party goers, resembling the crowd at Coachella. The entrance line was so long, I assumed we would make it inside when the shows were over for the day.

To distract myself from the impatience growing inside, I checked my emails until we were admitted, then called Mash to let him know I was there. My call went straight to voicemail, and I was torn if I should call again, fearing I was interrupting, or worse, being blown off.

The day was quickly slipping away, from the long line to enter the parking lot, the hours waiting in line to get inside, then the half hour walk to the main stage. A few of us didn't care to watch the concert from far away, or on the mega screens. Instead we split into pairs, doing as we pleased until ten o'clock.

Khai partnered with me to explore the grounds, but not because of shared interest. She was eager to meet the mystery man who had me smiling all morning.

We watched a few artists perform we had never heard of, had our horoscopes read for fun, and undoubtedly had a contact high from the marijuana swarming the gardens.

Hours later, I grew anxious to be in Mash's company. Khai and I footed the fields, until we found the tent Mash was scheduled to perform in. My palms grew sweaty as I texted him.

N: *I'm outside.*

He responded seconds later.

M: *Come to the back of the tent by the loading truck.*

We entered through the slim drapery next to a generator. Eyes from every direction were upon us, as we stood in front of two huge security guards. "Nadia!" shouted a voice to our right. "They are with us!" Prano yelled to the guards letting us pass.

The backstage crowd stared at us as we walked over to the seating area, as if they could tell we were foreigners without hearing us speak. A bad habit I had since childhood reappeared while working through the crowd. I began mocking a horrible impression of a British accent, saying "Pardon me," as I swept through the onlookers.

He kissed my cheek and my chest pounded fast and hard. My eyes twitched from nervousness, and as his hand wrapped around my waist, I nearly melted from his touch. The way he looked at me, made me feel desirable. I feared I could lose control with him. Be wild and carefree without remorse. *'So unlike me.'*

To break his spell, I ruined the moment by blurting out, "What is your real name?"

"Maximus Sharper," he answered, leading me to a sofa behind a curtain.

'Mmm, a strong name.'

My left leg crossed his right leg when we squeezed tightly in the corner of the couch, leaving plenty of space for Khai and Prano.

"And your surname is?" he asked.

"Melton."

"Melton? I don't think I know any Melton's." He clutched onto my hand placed on my thigh, running circles on my leg with his other.

Khai glanced from the corner of her eyes, then raised her eyebrows at me allowing him to fondle my skin. I smirked, letting her know I saw her reaction, then carried on with my conversation.

"So, did you dream about me?"

"I dreamt about our kiss. Is it too soon for another one?" He leaned in and smiled.

"No sir."

He pulled me in close by my shirt, and lightly swept his fingers around the back of my neck. Planting his luscious lips against mine, I gulped in his air as he took in mine, unapologetic for our public display of affection. Like a schoolgirl, I began counting the seconds not knowing when to pull back.

This kiss was hotter and longer than the one from the morning. Heat sparked between us, as neither he nor I showed signs of letting up. My knees were now in his lap, and both of my arms wrapped around him.

Khai interrupted us by clearing her throat a few times. "I'm Khai by the way."

I wiped my lipstick from his lips, and giggled. We turned towards my good friend, and I formally introduced her to the man of the hour.

"I haven't seen you smile like this in a long time," said Khai. "All is forgiven. Nice to meet you. Prano and I are going to give you two some privacy, but not too much." She joked.

"I promise I will behave." Mash held up his hands.

When Prano and Khai disappeared behind the curtain, Mash and I shared a laughable lip embrace, then cooled things down.

We conversed with the twenty minutes of free time he had remaining before his show. Our words connected like a game of scrabble. Our energy flowed in sync. The chemistry between us was explosive, and magic felt present when I was near him.

Time flew by so fast, it seemed like we had been talking for only a few minutes instead of twenty. The show coordinator called for him, and our lips touched once more.

"Have dinner with me tomorrow night?" His hands stroked my cheek.

Looking into his eyes, I envisioned being pressed beneath him with expressions of joy on my face. I could look into his eyes for days, nights even, and listen to him talk for hours.

His accent drove me wild, and the five o'clock shadow filling in on his face, reeled me further into his abyss. The longer I looked at him, the wilder my thoughts ran. "What time should I be ready?" I answered.

"Pick you up at seven."

For a moment, I contemplated hanging back until his set was complete, but we travel in packs for safety. I couldn't abandon Khai, nor did I want to look like a stage five clinger.

I argued with myself. *'He didn't ask you to hang back. Let him take you on a date and get wined and dined.'*

He walked me to the side of the stage, where I joined Khai and Prano. We watched him work for a while, then trekked back to the meeting point. Bypassing concerts in session, parties, tents and kiosks throughout the fairgrounds, we spent just as much time walking as we did watching shows.

Large crowds accosted us, carrying us away in their flock. We held hands to prevent being separated, as painted faces screaming and circling about, frightened us while trapped. The increasing size and weirdness of the crowd grew every second. Slightly worried, I drew in closer to Khai, and fought our way out of the drunken horde, safely returning to the meeting point.

The rest of our party regrouped, and Tony drove us back to the city. After a long flight, a night out, a catnap, a long drive, and the long day at the festival, I was exhausted. I slept on the bus, and throughout Sunday morning. Even after skipping breakfast and brunch, and spending the afternoon in bed, I was still physically tired, but found energy to get ready for my date with Mr. Sharper.

I didn't trust myself around him. I was participating in public displays of affection, and kissing him like I had known him longer than three days. The more I realized how reckless I was behaving, I was glad Khai and I chose to share room expenses. If I had a room to myself, I felt certain both of my feet would have been off of the floor before our date.

Preparing for this date became a strategic exercise. The dress I originally planned on wearing was overly, sexually enticing. Without a clue of where I was being taken, I opted to wear a blue one-piece jumpsuit instead. It had an open neckline which accentuated my healthy bosoms, then loosened as it left my curves down to the hem.

Since this was a special occasion, I accessorized with my custom Billie Hilliard bracelet cuffs, but only wore three-inch strappy heels for comfort. I placed my flat shoes in my oversized purse, and when Khai wasn't looking, added my toothbrush, a pair of panties, some leggings, and my make-up bag.

Maximus knocked on the door, and my heart fluttered. I felt like a teenage girl going on her first date, and lost all of my cool knowing he was on the other side of the door.

Before answering, I made a mental note to be as quiet as possible, and not say anything stupid.

I opened the door. "Damn," I mumbled.

"I'm sorry." He grinned.

His light brown eyes glistened as he greeted me with a single red rose and kiss on the cheek. I recovered my verbal fumble with, "Huh, oh nothing. I was talking to myself."

'I'm already muttering like an idiot.'

My mind betrayed me and let my tongue speak what I was thinking. I couldn't help myself. The man was fine as hell, and handsome as ever.

We hugged, long enough for me to sniff the orange notes of his cologne which blended well with his natural scent of take me now.

"Shall we?" He took me by the arm.

I clung to his manliness, admiring the sharp way he was dressed. His garments looked tailored. Fitted black slacks and a black pullover, with a light blue and black oxford shirt peeking at the collar.

I held on to him so tight, I knew he could tell I didn't want to let go when the elevator arrived. I was already smitten, picturing myself stroking his freshly trimmed beard, while looking up at him on the bed fucking me slow. Thank God Khai was there to block me from spreading wide eagle.

She liked Mash from the short time she spent with him, but still didn't trust the fact we were not on home soil. She made me promise to ping her my location every hour. Being married to a cop, she felt forced to share the safety tips Brian, her husband, taught her. But I wasn't worried. Foolish, maybe. Lustful, indeed. But not worried.

Mr. Sharper demonstrated what I never experienced in a grown man. He escorted me around his city in a vintage town car, made eye contact with me when speaking, placed his hand in the small of my back frequently, and held a full conversation while explaining the significance of well-known tourist attractions.

At dinner, he pulled out my chair, stood when I left the table, and didn't laugh as I wanted to try fish and chips at the upscale establishment. He ordered it as an appetizer after insisting I try his favorite dish, and I admired how he took charge, just as he did our first kiss.

Afraid I was going to humiliate myself, or say something stupid again, I kept quiet at dinner, creating an awkward vibe. He began to grow uncomfortable, and I couldn't pretend any longer, so I admitted what I was doing in an effort to lighten the mood.

He laughed at my honesty and confessed, he thought he had done something to offend me which caused me to withdraw.

The tension left the table and our vibe returned to normal,

as I began talking his head off. Telling him about my failed career attempts, my childhood dream of becoming a famous dancer, and how I now hoped to become a successful writer.

He listened to me ramble while stuffing my face in between, then I revealed what was really on my mind. I told him he was the first white guy I ever kissed, and went on a date with.

He sat pensively after my revelation, and I grew worried I had blown it by being too direct. I suffered as he sat in silence, looking at his near empty plate, fumbling his fingers against the white tablecloth.

I looked away as there was no eye contact between us, then he spoke. "I wanted to carefully craft what I am about to say. I'm flattered to be the first white guy you have spent time with. If I may ask, what took you so long?"

"I. I..." I stammered, choking on my words.

"I'm just joking. But in all seriousness, I would like to know why you gave me a chance?"

"It seems strange saying this, but there is something about you I can't explain. I wish I could articulate what I want to say better, but for some reason I can't. It's like there are no words to describe it, but it exists. I probably sound crazy right now."

"Actually, you don't. I know exactly what you are trying to say." He smiled at me with his eyes.

I swirled the wine in front of my lips, sniffed and sipped slowly. I returned his stare and confessed. "I've received offers outside of my race before, but I never felt compelled to accept. Until now. You are the first I've ever been attracted to."

"Are you comfortable being out with me?" he asked.

"Are you comfortable being seen with me?"

"Why wouldn't I be? You're beautiful. And since we are talking about this, you may as well know, I have gone out with women of all persuasions, but you are the first to have this effect on me."

'Same.'

I was in trouble, falling fast and hard, and worried about the future instead of enjoying the present. Terrified my heart was going to get broken. In the back of my mind, I thought the only thing that could save me, was if the rumor about British men being horrible lovers turned out to be true. He had no idea, but I knew I was going to find out the answer to that question tonight.

The amount of food we ordered was gluttonous. Maximus suggested we take an after-dinner stroll to walk some of it off, and led me down a few lesser crowded streets.

The sound of traffic surrounded us as we walked a few blocks, and ended up in a courtyard across from Buckingham Palace. The gold and white lights lit the site so bright, I could see it clearly from where we stood.

He placed his jacket around my sweater, as the night air turned on its chill, staring at me marvel at the historic palace. The glimmer in my eyes lured him in, and we found ourselves kissing in the moonlight, wanting more of one another, and not wanting the night to end.

"Are you ready to go back to the hotel?" he asked.

"No. But if you need to get some rest I understand."

"Rest is the last thing on my mind." He traced my hand with his fingers, and gazed into my eyes.

"So where to then?"

"I'd love to show you my place?"

"I'd love to see it."

We drove a little under an hour from the city into the suburbs. Curvy roads, dark streets, and many hillsides later, Mash entered a code into a gated community, with at least three acres between each home in a dimly lit neighborhood.

The houses were huge, and I grew anxious to see where we were going to end up.

He pulled into this beautiful mini castle like home, with mild lighting outside its exterior, and greenery for days. I thought to myself, *'He must be one hell of a deejay to afford something of this nature.'*

It was intimidating. My small three-bedroom starter home could fit inside this colossal house. I felt out of my league and became quiet again, shifting back into awkwardness.

My silence was broken when Mash asked me what I thought about his house. I thought it was a lot of house for one person, but I didn't dare say it aloud. "I love it. It's beautiful." I smiled.

"Thank you. I was thinking of downsizing next year, but I like the area."

"I admire your taste. Did you do the interior design?" I inquired.

"I hired professionals. I couldn't pull all of this off."

"Well they did an excellent job. It's clean and modern, but most importantly it reflects a man lives here. It's sexy."

"Come on, let me show you around."

He began the tour with his man cave/studio, where he housed all of his collectible toys, a bar for hosting, and a Styrofoam room where he recorded his music. We then walked into each of the five bedrooms and workout area near the living room.

Along the walls were mounted abstract paintings and nothing personal. Floating shelves, but no pictures of a mother, child, or himself. Only paintings and random wall decorum, of what I perceived as an expensive Indian collection.

Next, we entered the living room where a massive, curved screen television rose from the floor. I acted impressed but I wasn't. All men seem to be fascinated with oversized TVs, and the latest electronic gadget.

Below it was an electric fireplace I desperately wished he turned on. The house was beautiful but nippy, and I was hoping this would be the room we lounged in, so I could get warm in front of the fire.

I pulled my sweater closer together and hoped he noticed. I thought he did when he took one of the decorative fur throws from the sofa, and wrapped it around me. I was wrong. He covered me so we could climb five steps from the left side of the living room, where he led me through a double glass door to an outside pool area.

I couldn't see the landscape, but I imagined it was beautiful. We cuddled under the fur blanket, admiring the stars in the sky as the moon's reflection hit the waves in the pool.

We conversed about music, movies, our likes and dislikes, and cultural differences without checking the time, which moved on significantly.

"I have an important question to ask you." His tone of voice turned serious. "What is your favorite song of all time?"

"Ugh, that's a hard one. I love so many different genres."

"But there has to be one song you love more than any other piece of music. When I asked the question, what song popped into your head?"

"Sting, *When We Dance*," I professed.

"Voila, your favorite song of all time."

"I do love it. It's definitely in my top five. What's your favorite song?"

"Bob Marley, *Waiting in Vain*."

"Ooh, another good one."

"It is, isn't it?

A breeze of cold air infiltrated the blanket. I shivered and drew closer to him, pressing my head against his chest for warmth. He squeezed my shoulders, and I relaxed— nestled next to him.

"I'm assuming you like reggae music from the other night." He grinned to himself.

"Very much so."

"What's your favorite Bob song?"

"*Chances Are*."

"You surprise me." He scoffed.

"Why?"

"I thought you were going to name a more commercial, more well-known one by The Great Late."

I had run out of words, and silence found its way back in as we stared at each other, wondering what the other was thinking. He took me by the face and kissed me so tender I felt a tingle in my chest.

"You're freezing." He rubbed the coldness of my cheeks. "Let's go inside."

He led me to the stone colored rug in front of the fireplace. With the flip of a switch, the black glass revealed a red and brown fire behind the panel. We canoodled in front of it until the blanket was no longer needed, continuing the tender kiss he planted on me outside. My sweater was tossed, then his sweater disappeared, as the heat from the fire, and from us, sweltered the room.

He let me unbutton half of his oxford shirt, while fighting the urge to explore me with his hands. I found his restraint admirable, but I knew he wanted to ravish me, so I played his game and stopped undressing him. "You didn't finish giving me the tour," I said, punishing him.

He rose to his feet and helped me off of the rug, holding my hand as he escorted me to the kitchen. I noticed him looking at me, then looking away when I caught him.

I laughed to myself, wishing I could read his mind. Imagining the conversation he was having in his head, since I pulled the brakes in the living room. *'I just couldn't be a cliché giving it up on his living room floor.'*

He paused in the hallway and pressed me against the wall. Stealing a few soft kisses, and running his fingers up and down my arm. I wanted to shout, *Take me!* Instead, I held it together as the intensity continued to build.

"Why don't you have any pictures on your walls?" I distracted him.

He backed away, still holding my hands and replied, "I thought photographs belonged in photo albums, not walls."

"Okay," I said, feeling I had overstepped.

"Whose picture should be hanging around?" he asked.

"Um your parents, or one of you mixing, or one of your favorite moments maybe." I responded and questioned at the same time.

"Maybe I will. I hadn't put much thought into it. I'd be happy to share my photo albums with you if you want."

I didn't answer. I motioned my head to the room up ahead, then led him towards it. "What a kitchen!"

"I have used the stove maybe twice, and I've never used the oven." He snarked.

"Seriously? I could get fat in a kitchen like this. You have everything. I mean literally everything."

"Yeah, but it's no fun cooking for one." His eyes followed me.

"So true. I cook and invite my crew over to eat all the time."

"So, you cook a lot?"

"Cook and bake."

"I hope I get invited to one of those dinners. I'd like to see you in action."

"Trust, I can burn."

"You can what?" He scowled.

"Burn. Where I'm from it means I cook really well. Slang or Ebonics is what some would call it. I might whip up something for you while I'm here. Ugh, do I spy another pool table in your dining room?"

"And that brings us to the last room in the house."

Adjacent to the kitchen was an obvious dining room, where a second pool table sat in place of a dining table. I felt I had already pried, when I asked about the pictures, so I waited for him to volunteer, why he designed his fine china room so poorly.

Circling the table while eyeing him with suspicion, I waited for an explanation. He played my game as I ran from him, making him chase me, then he caved.

"Yes, there is a table downstairs, but what can I say. I love the game. It is my favorite pastime, and my stress reliever. Sometimes I don't want to walk all the way downstairs, so I put another table in this empty space," he said proudly.

"You don't owe me any explanations about your house, but the fact you did has earned you some bonus points. I think it's cute. Plus, it is still a table, right?"

"Right. I knew you were smart. You get it. But uh, I didn't know I needed bonus points." He closed in on me. "You're the first person to ever walk through my entire house."

"Yeah right." I tapped his shoulder. "I'm not calling you a liar, but that just seems a bit far-fetched. I mean come on. A house this beautiful? It's hard to believe no one in your life has ever walked down these halls."

"It's true. I've been here a month or two, over a year and you are the first."

I couldn't look him in the eye. It was hard to believe he hadn't had a woman stay over, and roam his house for a night or a weekend. Looking away, I used his same words from dinner.

"Why me?"

"I wish I knew why I chose you to be the first. I know I'm definitely vibing with you," he answered.

"I'm feeling you as well."

"Ah! She said she's feeling me," he said aloud. "So it's mutual then?"

"It seems so."

This would have been the perfect time to be a mind reader. How could I really know Mr. Sharper wasn't playing with my emotions? I was really enjoying his company, and getting to know him and the world he lived in.

He was smooth, and I couldn't tell if he was being pretentious with me. Those sweet, tantalizing kisses we shared had me wanting to explore him below the surface, and I was too far gone to know, if he masterfully played me like a game of chess. "When will I get to see your house?" he asked.

And there it was. The second reference of coming to visit me. '*God, I hope he is for real.*'

"My house? It's nothing like this. It's cozy, and clean and decorated to my taste, but it's nothing compared to yours. Would you really come to the States to see me?" I leaned back to look him straight in the eyes.

"I'm already planning it in my head."

"You're serious, aren't you?"

"I say what I mean, and I mean what I say. I told you at dinner, I felt a connection with you the moment I saw you. I couldn't take my eyes off of you. Watching you move, was the only reason I let the song you were dancing to, play all the way through. I didn't want you to stop dancing, or for it to be the last time I saw you. No one has ever had that effect on me before. Ever."

"I haven't felt close to anyone for a few years now," I confessed.

"What about right now?"

"Right now, I'm feeling like a teenager. Do you remember the tingling feeling you'd get when your crush would walk by you in the hallway, or look your way?"

"I do. My crush is standing before me, and I'm feeling a tingling sensation looking at her."

"You've been feeling a sensation of some sort for most of the night." I teased him.

"I've traveled many places Nadia. I've seen many world beauties, but none have measured up to you."

"What if it's just lust?"

"I'm definitely lusting you, but I'm also falling in love with you. I'm a firm believer when you know you know," he said, towering over me.

I failed searching for the truth in his eyes. I stared in them and became blinded by a combination of lust, desire, and naivety. I clung to every word he uttered, believing his words were honest and pure.

"Will you let me love you?" he said, now molding my chin with his fingers, and nibbling my lips.

"Love me or fuck me?" I sighed, desperately wanting his kisses to continue, and they did up and down my neck.

He slipped his fingers between my breasts, slowly unzipping my suit. "Both."

And there was the smoothness again. '*This is too soon for this to be love. Right? It would be insane to let this man fuck me after three days. Right?*'

We knew a little about each other— but I still couldn't resist the physical desire exploding inside of me. I wanted him. Bad. Badly. Properly. Now. Nervously, I shuttered as he removed the straps from my shoulders, still seducing me with his gaze. His hands began to stroke the top lining of my bra, and my senses heightened from his gentle touch— almost giving me the healing of reiki, but not yet quite there.

I took his hand and placed it over my racing heart, so he could feel his effect on me. He grinned, then delicately whispered in my ear, "May I touch you?" in the deepest, most virile tone.

I became heavily lubricated— there was no need for foreplay. I melted into his grasp as I felt the hook of my bra become unfastened. He stood back, and waited for it to fall onto the floor giving me a once over, then smirked on the side of his mouth.

He had me on display, studying every inch of my topless body. "I'm going to remove those now." He pointed to my tangas.

"Okay." I sighed, as he stepped back towards me, fell to his knees, and slid his fingers between my hips, pulling my panties to my feet.

As before, he examined me, but this time I was fully naked, and could feel his hungry breath upon my navel. I trembled as he read me, giving him my power, and closed my eyes awaiting his next move.

One ankle lifted, then the other, as I quivered from the anticipation of what was to come. Suddenly, I felt the presence of his fingers upon me. They were warm, feeling the curves of my buttocks and exterior of my walls.

Quickly, he jerked his hands and pulled me closer to his face, where he landed the softest kiss on my lips down below. My eyes opened, and I looked down to see the bottom half of his face, missing in between my legs. "Aye Papi," I muttered.

Not only was this man causing my pussy to pulsate, he now had me speaking in random Spanish.

I ran my fingers across his head while he held me in position, then balanced me on one leg, placing the other across his shoulder, never skipping a beat on his tongue service.

I occasionally enjoyed a good licking down below, but it was never an act I required. Thanks to Mr. Sharper, my position was rapidly changing about foreplay as I, for the first time, quavered and released from oral stimulation.

This new lover of mine, was undeniably experienced in tongue play, and had to have sensed I was about to come. As soon as my body began to trill, he stuck his finger on my clitoris, and applied pressure, while generously open mouthed kissed me from my navel to my breasts.

He lingered there for at least a minute, sucking on my nipples until he finally released his finger from my trigger spot. "So, you speak Spanish?" he asked, rising to stand on his feet, then wiped his mouth with his shirt.

Not an inch of fat was on his abs. The black and brown stubble on his chest begged me to kiss them. I did so softly before answering with what little voice I could find.

"Not really. I don't know where that came from."

He flashed his whites at me. "I think you're ready for me."

I nodded yes as he steered me towards the wall where he lifted my thighs with his wrists, and placed his wood against my crevice. I heard plastic crumbling, and smelled the latex as he drew back, and rolled the condom down until it smacked. *'Thank goodness we didn't have to have that talk,'* I thought to myself as I sighed at the pressure, neglecting to look at his package.

I'd never seen an ivory cock in person before, but I was about to feel one. My shoulders tensed and my back locked at his first attempt to enter. "Breathe," he commanded. I didn't realize I was holding my breath, but Mash was paying close attention to me, and could feel me tense up upon his entry. I obeyed and exhaled. "There you go. You can take it. Good girl."

He sultrily coached me as I gripped him inside my walls. "Hold on to me." He warned before feeding me to the wall, leaving my imprint in the indigo cracks.

Back and forth, up and down, fast then slow, he stroked without any struggle to lift my body midair. He moaned and complimented how good I felt to him, as I held on for dear life, just as he instructed.

Tightly gripping my arms around his neck and atop his shoulders, I was panting with delight and moaning in his ear. "Maximus, Maximus."

The sound of my voice made him thrust deeper and deeper. I was in mind-blowing ecstasy and taking the full beating, pinned between him and the wall with no way out. Mash was heavily endowed and possibly ruining me, but I was loving it. No one could top this performance and he knew it. He was owning me. Staking his claim. Planting his flag in my life box.

My shyness faded the more I pulsated in his clutch, and I pulled his head back so I could finally make eye contact with him. He liked I was finally engaging, and not letting him be the only aggressor, grunting slightly louder, showing me his sexy grin, and kissing me fervidly, but slower than the motion he was grinding.

His attentiveness to hit every corner made me spasm, and our eyes connected as I arrived at orgasm number two.

As I rained on him, he switched his movement to subtle, long strokes. Applying the pressure I needed to get it all out. "You okay?" He removed himself.

"I am more than okay." I whined. "Did you?"

"I held it back. I'm not done with you yet." He delivered a swift kiss to my lips, then took me by the hand.

He led me over to the pool table in the dining room. I could barely lift my feet to follow him, but somehow managed to in my weak state. Without any more chatter, he turned my back to him and positioned me up against the table, placing one of my feet in the ball socket while the other remained on the floor.

He kissed the back of my neck with an open mouth, then lower, and lower, surprising me with a sudden insertion to my warmth.

I screeched and grabbed onto the green velvet, accepting his entrance while listening to him enjoy me. "Nadia, you feel so damn good." He groaned.

Mash was relishing in my body, my juice, my lines— and I was pleased to please him, enduring all he had to give. The pain and the pleasure were a lot to handle, but the sensation of his hands massaging my back, and the tugging of my hips, enthralled me with levels of pleasure I never imagined.

From this angle, he waxed my ass like he was the karate kid, until he segmentally arched my back from pulling my hair, lifting my head off of the green velvet and let loose.

It felt like thunder, though thunder can only be heard. His exhalation was boisterous, assuring me his reveling inside my love, would classify tonight as one he would never forget.

I lied motionless with him still inside of me, waiting for release. My shoulders slumped from pure relaxation, and a good sleep working its way in. Maximus pardoned my body, and I turned around to look at him, and to look at it.

I was mesmerized. It was tawny and wider than I had ever witnessed, longer than average, and absolutely perfect. I looked up at his face, then back at it once more, unable to look away.

"You made quite a mess."

"I had some help."

He stepped away into the kitchen and discarded the rubber. He returned with two bottles of water, as I stood not knowing what to do with myself. He sat me on the edge of the table, positioned between my legs.

Caressing my back as I sipped, I wilted in his arms. "Come on, let's take a shower and go to bed." He carried me to the master bedroom, and sat me in the middle of the black marbled double vanity.

Once the steam rose from the running water, I cleansed his scent off of me, while he gathered my clothing scattered all over the house. When I was done he wrapped me in a towel, and escorted me to his bed where he had a t-shirt laid out for me. He pulled the sheets back and I climbed in, waiting for him to join me, sleepy and unable to get comfortable in the unfamiliar setting.

When he was finally next to me, he sat up fumbling through his phone. Mine buzzed nonstop in my bag, and for some reason I asked permission to answer.

We looked at each other, both confused by the question. I answered Khai on Facetime, ready for my lashing.

"It's good to know you are okay," she said.

"I know I forgot to ping you." I stretched my bottom lip then smiled.

"Why the hell are you smiling so big? And are you lying down? And where is your make-up?" She grilled me.

"I only answered the phone so you could see I am okay. I'll talk to you later."

"And you are glowing! Where is Mr. Maximus?!"

"He's right here."

"Hi Khai," Mash said in the background.

"You are alright with me Maximus!" Khai cackled.

"Good night." I urged.

"I guess this means you aren't going with us to Paris in the morning?"

"No, I'll have to miss Paris. Bring me a chocolate croissant please."

"I most definitely will. Talk with you tomorrow."

"Good night Khai." Mash added.

"Good night fornicators." Khai laughed.

We laughed at being called fornicators for a good minute. "Are you okay with missing Paris to hang out with me?" He kissed the back of my hand.

"Yeah it's cool. I really wanted to go to Ibiza anyway."

"Ibiza? Why?"

"I'm fascinated with the big mythical rock Es Vedra."

"I've had a few shows out there and never paid any attention to it. I've definitely heard about it, but my visits were mostly work related."

"People say they can feel an energy from it. I was just curious to see it, and feel it for myself."

"Well I'll make tomorrow worth your while since I'm interrupting your plans." He squeezed my hand.

"You're a good interruption. I have no complaints."

He leaned over and told me to check my phone. A copy of his schedule for the week, highlighting the days and time he would be free during my visit, sat in my inbox.

He then invited me to join him in Paris for a show on Friday. I reminded him I had obligations, and would have to miss his show because of the rehearsal dinner.

"I keep forgetting you are here for a wedding. Sooooo, I guess I'll see you at, or after the wedding? If I'm invited?"

"You can be my plus one, and you better not stand me up." I gave him a stern eye.

"Ha! She's bossing me now."

"What I meant to say was, I'd love for you to be my plus one."

"I thought you'd never ask."

CHAPTER 4
TASTE

The clock read 4 a.m. and I was wide awake. Under normal circumstances, I would be fast asleep at this hour. Alone or wishing I was alone. My thoughts were running rampant, and my body was growing impatient for those thoughts to come to fruition.

Lying still on my back in the middle of the bed, I was trapped under one arm and afraid to move. My eyes wandered from left to right, searching for clues and details he hadn't shared, or may have wanted to keep hidden.

His room was neat and well organized. Everything was in place from what I could see. The pillows on the lounge correctly tucked down the middle.

The marble abstract piece, properly placed in the center of the nightstand next to a book and a lamp. And all dust free. I could only assume he hired a maid service for the upkeep, or he had a girlfriend he neglected to mention. *'Don't go down that road,'* I thought, but it was too late. The can of worms had been opened, and I wasn't going to be able to get it out of my head, unless I went back to sleep.

I closed my eyes and listened to Mash sleeping peacefully next to me. Instead of joining him, my mind continued to race — reminiscing how good I felt up against the wall in the kitchen, to imagining him with other women, then I coughed. He twisted a few times, finally releasing me from his hold, and I turned on my side away from him and pretended to be asleep.

He slid closer to me, and from behind whispered in my ear in a deep, groggy voice. "Is something wrong?"

"No," I lied. "How did you know I was awake?"

"I felt you move. Are you comfortable?" He kissed the back of my head.

"Yeah, I'm good."

"Tell me. What's on your mind?"

"Everything. Mainly the past three days, and how I ended up in your bed."

"You being in my bed isn't a bad thing I hope?"

"It certainly doesn't feel like a bad thing."

I was back in his embrace. His arm wrapped around my waist, and he stretched the t-shirt he gave me, to kiss the back of my shoulder.

"Then what's wrong?" he asked.

"There lies the problem. Nothing is wrong. I'm over here already thinking about Sunday— when I have to get on the plane to go home."

"Kotch. Don't think about Sunday."

"What does kotch mean?" I snickered.

"Relax."

"I'd like to, but something else is bothering me. I was also wondering who is going to be in this spot when I leave. Please, don't judge me for being jealous, when I have no right to be. I just got a little curious as to why you are single. I mean come on, there has to be someone keeping you company."

"If you are asking if I have a girlfriend, the answer is no. I have no reason to lie to you. I have a few friends I can call if I don't want to be alone, but nothing serious. And none of them have been in this bed."

"No offense, but I'm calling bullshit."

"I told you, I feel something for you I haven't with anyone else. I have other bedrooms, and yes, I have entertained in them, but never in here. This is my personal space. Why are we talking about this again?" He huffed.

"Because this is what I do. I overthink things, open my mouth, and everything goes to shit."

"I think you feel what I feel and you're scared. Admit it."

"I am a little scared."

"I have no intentions of hurting you. Do you believe me?"

I hesitated.

"Say you believe me." He pushed.

"I believe you."

"Now say you trust me."

"Nope."

He pressed firmly against my back, cocked and loaded, ready to strike. I had been lying awake, waiting for a second round. "Say it," he demanded, searching for my tickle spot.

"I said I believe you have no intentions of hurting me."

"Now say you trust me."

"Un uh." I screeched with laughter, until he silenced my giggles by sucking on my neck, mixed with tongue traces and gentle bites grazing my skin. "I trust you," I gasped.

He took a pause and smiled at me. Kissing me from my cheek, to below my chin, and then my shoulders he softly whispered, "You don't have to worry about anyone else."

I didn't believe him, though he was convincing, smiling at me in between kisses. His rod grew larger against my thighs, causing my papaya to *kegel*. Ready to wrinkle the sheets, my legs opened wide for him, ready for the taking, and grinded upwards hoping he would slide in.

Our eyes locked as he grabbed my bum, squeezing it like a stress ball. I removed the t-shirt he gave me, then begged him to put it inside. He touched me and grinned at the drip greeting him, then pressed his weaponry against my wetness.

"I want to feel the real you. May I?" he asked.

"Are you clean?" I sassed.

"Yes. I always use condoms, but I want to feel you skin on skin. You said you trust me."

"Don't make me regret this." I poked his chest.

"I promise I won't."

"Ah!" I sighed from the penetration.

"Breathe my love," he said, watching me welcome him. I exhaled as he held me tight around my waist, accelerating forward and fully inside, groaning at the sensation of pure flesh.

With my arms cuddled beneath him, the slow grind of push and pull ignited an awakening in me I couldn't fight. Him grunting against my chest, somehow made me feel even closer to him.

Tighter and tighter, I cradled his head against me, rocking back and forth in unison. He came up for air and I grazed my teeth against his shoulder, catching what he threw at me. His head lifted and our lips met for soft pecks, and quick compliments to one another.

"I love how I feel inside you," he whispered.

"I love how you feel inside me," I moaned.

"You're driving me insane woman."

He dove deeper and applied his lips to my forehead, swept my hair off of my face, then tugged it from the nape. Watching me turn into putty as he pummeled and massaged my head simultaneously, I drizzled on him, causing him to shriek.

"Messy girl," he taunted, then enhanced his strokes, intensifying my orgasm.

I screamed out, "Do whatever you want to me!"

And he did, taking it up a notch to next level shit, digging into me like crates. Wearing out his welcome with one of the toys he fancied in my box, he skillfully lifted my right leg, and flipped me over while still inside. I yelled, "Oh shit," as he went directly back into thrashing me from behind.

Lying flat on my stomach, I could feel every inch of him against the back of my canal. I had given him total control, and he proved I was now in his world. And I liked it here. I loved it here.

I clenched onto the pillows as he held me down by my shoulders, and worked me over, moving in circles, then pausing, then circles again. "Baby I'm close!" he shouted, "You are too much for me from the back!" And he climaxed animalistic this time, howling in delight, and panting as if he just completed a mile run.

Falling beside me he panted, smacking my ass, unable to speak. Seconds later he mumbled, "I have to meet this couple and thank them for bringing you to me."

I nestled close to him and slipped my feet beneath his, and finally lost the battle to a deep sleep.

UNAWARE OF THE HOUR, I felt a presence above me and opened my eyes. Mash was fully dressed standing over me, telling me to sleep in while he ran an errand. "Leave clean sheets," I muttered before drifting back into the darkness.

He hadn't returned by the time I fully woke. I rose from the soiled sheets, looked around his drawers to appease my curiosity, then jumped in the shower a second time.

I returned to the bed wrapped in a towel, changed the linens, and took advantage of thumbing through the photo albums, he left at the foot of the bed for my amusement.

The first book painted a colorful story of his teenage years. Pictures of him in a private school uniform, team sports, posing with album covers, and shadowing deejays, completed the first half section. The final portion displayed more moments of him carrying records, and what I assumed were girlfriends.

The next book was filled with old pictures of what had to be his family. Black and white portraits of beautiful people, which explained his striking looks. It dawned on me, we hadn't discussed our family history of where our ancestors hailed from. I made a mental note to bring it up in our conversation, if we experienced a dry moment.

Flipping through the second book led me to the conclusion he had an interesting story to tell. It became obvious he was more than a Brit, and I couldn't wait to hear what he revealed.

While reaching for the third book, I realized I was completely air dried. I dressed in the leggings and tee hidden away in my bag, then plopped back down on the bed to finish snooping.

This book was the most questionable, and impressive by far. A plethora of photographs with actors, athletes, singers, and models I recognized from runway shows and commercials.

Turning the pages, I was hit with multiple, beautiful women smiling back at me, which played my insecurities like a fiddle. I began to imagine some of them lying on the bed staring at me, smirking at my existence, teasing I didn't belong. I slammed the book shut, envious of the women who made it into his memorabilia. *'Everyone has a past,'* I said to myself, then snapped out of it.

The garage door hurled and roared, and I rushed to the

vanity to pull my hair back and fix my face. Mash walked in holding a small white paper bag in one hand, and shopping bags in the other. His face curled as he glanced up and down at my attire, then chuckled as he teased me. "You had plans of spending the night I see."

"I bet you're happy I did." I sassed.

"Fucking ecstatic."

His ego increased tenfold, without any signs of returning back to normal after discovering my secret. "I got you a few things, but it looks like you won't need all of them," he said, placing the shopping bags on a bench at the foot of the bed. He then handed me a pastry box from the small white one. "I'm sorry you missed Paris with your friends."

I opened the box. A freshly baked chocolate croissant with two strawberries, soothed my morning hunger as I pulled the flaky pastry apart. With a mouth full I chortled, "As you can see I was starving. And thank you. This is heavenly."

"Only the best for you."

"Where are my manners? Do you want some?"

"No thanks. I'm enjoying watching you have a go at it."

"Good. Because I really didn't want to share it."

I closed my eyes and bit into the last piece, savoring the flavors, while wishing he had brought two of them home. Licking the chocolate from my fingers, then chasing it with a strawberry, I pranced in my stance and nodded to Mash, motioning you did good.

He turned the shopping bags upside down, covering the bed with new tags, a box of flats, and an array of panties and matching bras. For reference, he took my clothes to a boutique, and brought back a few outfits for me to wear.

"Did you pick these out?" I asked.

"No. A friend did."

"Your friend has taste. So, was this the errand you had to run this morning?"

"Sort of. Get dressed. We're going to be late. I'll wait for you downstairs."

His assertiveness was attractive, but I began to wonder if I had given him too much control. I also wondered why I liked it so much. I was aware I could be naïve, but never had I been submissive, and did whatever I was told. *'Maybe he just wants to show me a good time while I'm here,'* I thought, as I popped the tags on a bohemian print skirt, solid magenta tee, and denim jacket.

I spruced up my make-up, threw on the flats, and off we went. A short twenty-minute ride further into the country, led us into an open-air field. *'Oh, Dear God! Please don't let him think he is about to fly me around in that thing. I'm already impressed! I'm already impressed!'*

Fright was written on my face, when a short elderly man appeared from the rear of a personal Beechcraft plane. "Park over there for me," he shouted, then tipped his hat.

I dragged getting out of the car, regretting I hadn't spoken my mind. As Mash opened my door, the gentleman walked over and shook hands with him, then extended them to me.

"Nice to meet you." He helped me out of the car.

"Nadia." I gave him my hand.

"Nadia, meet Mr. Hunt, a longtime friend of the family."

"And a pilot I hope." My brows raised.

"For thirty years now," Mr. Hunt asserted.

"Suddenly, I'm not so nervous anymore."

Mr. Hunt laughed, then escorted me over to the plane, while Mash gathered bags he had stashed in the trunk. The steps lowered and we boarded, receiving a full tutorial on safety and emergency information, and what if scenarios.

I gripped the edge of my seat at takeoff, counting the

minutes until we were settled in the air. Searching for a distraction, I pestered Mash to tell me where we were going, but he remained tight lipped.

He dug into the bags and pulled out a Sudoku book, pencils, a mystery novel he hadn't finished, and a bag of chips — offering me each of the items, refusing to answer my question.

The plane leveled in the sky moments later, and I released the arm rests from my clutch. Mash gave me a cocky once over, then tapped my hand. "We'll be there in a few hours. Sit tight and enjoy the scenery."

I stared at him without blinking for a few seconds, attempting to read his mind. His poker face was stern as he circled words in the book, and so I gave up and did as he suggested. I sat back, pulled my earpiece from my purse, and listened to my calm playlist. *'I bet he's taking me to Paris to meet my friends.'*

An hour into the flight I grew bored and anxious. I leaned over and helped solve a few puzzles, read some of his book, then asked him to give me a list of the songs he produced.

We shared our playlists from our phones, and he complimented my arrangements and selections, "You have open ears. I've never seen a playlist like this before. You went from Kings of Leon to Nina Simone, Coldplay, OutKast, Prince, Edie Brickell, Fiona and Jay-Z in your shuffle file."

"You'll love my Texas rap on there, too," I added.

"Why is it called Texas rap, and not just rap?"

"Because of how it sounds, and how it flows. They call it chopped and screwed. Stick with me kid, you'll learn something new." I clicked my tongue.

I played him a few songs from Houston artists. His reaction was priceless, having never heard a record chopped and screwed before. I looked on as he took it all in, and assumed he was contemplating new ideas from the way his lips mouthed words to himself.

When he removed his headset, I pried into his business. "Do you care to discuss the photo albums?"

He turned his head and scoffed. "I was wondering when you'd bring that up."

"So, private school?"

"Yes. My mother is Italian and my father is full Brit. My dad raised me after they divorced. He came from wealth and believed my mother couldn't make me become a man, plus he had control of the money, so you know how that goes. He wanted me to be the next big thing. Forcing me to try my hand in everything he liked. Soccer, Lacrosse, Tennis, Rugby, Polo, Boxing.

'That explains the body.'

"Did you like any of those sports?" I asked.

"I was into boxing— up until I was knocked out. I continued training, but stopped sparring. Anyway, my interests didn't matter to my father. I was always attracted to music, but he didn't approve. I had to sneak around in clubs, and learn how to work turntables, speakers and mixing boards. When I went off to university, I made a name for myself on campus."

"And look at you now. He must be proud."

"He wasn't around long enough to see me get to this level. He passed away."

Maximus turned his away and stared out of the window. I met eyes with Mr. Hunt watching us in her rearview mirror.

"Sorry to hear that. My dad passed away three years ago. It's an experience you'll never get over."

"Losing someone you love, when the relationship was full of turmoil, is even worse. But you can't change a person, so it is what it is."

"There it is!" Mr. Hunt yelled.

I wobbled to the closest window, prepared to see the Eiffel Tower from the best view possible. During our quiet time, I put two and two together. The croissant was a clue I assumed, so I braced myself for the big reveal. "What the!" I screeched, looking at miles and miles of turquoise water leading the way to the magical rock, Es Vedra in the distance.

"You brought me to see the rock! I'm in Ibiza! The Baleares Islands of Spain! I can't fucking believe it! Excuse my language. Holy shit! I didn't think I was going to see this place!" I exclaimed.

"You were so close, and the way your face lit up talking about it, I figured I owed it to you, since you know. You missed Paris."

"I thought you were taking me to Paris to meet my friends, hence the breakfast croissant, but this is so much better! I can't believe you did this for me."

A black line dripped from the corner of my eye. I fought to hold my tears, but one resisted flowing back into my glands and exposed itself.

"Come here," Mash said, reaching for me.

I returned to my seat.

"Buckle up sweetheart, we are about to land," said Mr. Hunt.

Carried away with emotion, I became putty sitting next to Mash. We kissed, necked, caressed and rubbed, becoming aroused at an inopportune time.

The decline disturbed our moment. "I can never repay you." The glee I felt inside spread across my face.

"Your excitement was repayment enough," he said.

My feet touched the soil of Spain. My skin felt the breath of the calm water surrounding Es Vedra. My eyes magnified a landscape of beauty. My nose inhaled the scent of the crisp trees spritzed in the air, and without making it to the beach, I was already in love with the place.

Four hours were spared to tour, and explore the historical city. For starters, we shopped at the many outposts, where I found an array of organic oils and beauty products. Some of the brands were familiar, and the others I came to know.

After buying more than enough goodies, we taxied to the white sandy beach of Cala d'Hort, and dined at Restaurante Es Boldado. The mysterious rock Es Vedra sat beautifully in the view, making me anxious to take a stroll near the water before high tide.

As the sand on the beach invaded my sandals, I soaked in the energy of the magnetic rock I had been dreaming to visit. Mash stood at my side, watching me take it all in.

Meditating with my eyes closed. Listening to the waves crash and burn. Its presence was majestic and commanding, and everything I hoped it would be. Calming yet thought provoking of its existence, mystifying and legendary, wondrous and extraordinary.

We wandered until we reached the famous tower, Torre des Savinar. It was rumored to be the best place to witness the sunset, and from what we experienced I could concur. The skyline melded from sapphire to bloodshot, as the sun slowly declined into the water, captivating us both.

A peacefulness flowed within me, as Mash was draped his arms around me from behind, gripping my waist, stealing kisses on my neck. The burning ball in the navy sky began its journey to the other side of the world, and a familiar feeling cloaked my chest. I was overcome with emotion, overwhelmed from the perfect past couple of days, and overjoyed to be in the company of a man who made me feel wanted. "Do you feel that?" I asked.

"I do." He pecked my cheek.

"I can't explain it. It's so beautiful, and so, I, I..."

"Sometimes there are no words."

But there were words. I just couldn't say it. I wanted to, but I was being cautious, and mildly childish not wanting to be the first to say I love you— as if it mattered.

'Why would it matter who said it first? If it's real, it's real.'

Maximus chose action over words and planted his saccharine lips on mine as a breeze of cool wind trapped us, sending chills over my body and up my skirt.

"It's time to go home," he said.

I smiled into his glimmering brown eyes. "I like the way that sounds."

"What do you like about it?" He grinned.

"The home part," I said, kissing him one last time under the heavenly sky.

'Ugh why couldn't I say it?'

Mr. Hunt delivered us safely to the London countryside. The hours crept by slowly, making my urge to physically thank Mash unbearable. Once we landed, I waited for him in the car as he settled business with his longtime friend, yearning to show my gratitude. Watching his lips move as he talked, I grew profoundly aroused, slipping my panties off, and placing them in my jacket pocket before he made it to the car.

As he drove us back to his place, I brushed my hand in his hair, and stared at him handling the curves of the road. When the path straightened, I took my panties out of my pocket, and dropped them in his lap.

"When did you...?" he asked.

"Pull over," I said, unzipping his pants.

The car jerked to the side of a dirt path, near bushes

leading to the woods. His wood stood at attention, as I slid his trousers down a few inches, and marveled at it, rubbing it in the dim moonlight escaping through the clouds. It was the color of roasted red pepper hummus, longer than average, and wide like a mushroom at the top.

'*No wonder I'm swooning.*'

In excitement, he neglected to put the gear in park, and the car rolled a few feet. After shifting it correctly, he turned off the engine, then I grabbed him by the face and kissed him, short but forcefully.

Pulling away I purred. "Un uh. Allow me," I offered, while shoving him back against the seat before I dove.

He huffed at the touch of my jaws, wet and slippery, cupping him whole inside of my mouth. He moaned and called out, "Nadia," as I teased him at the tip with my tongue, then held him at the roof of my mouth, swirling my tongue in circles.

His moans deepened from the oral massage as I sped up the pace, up and down nonstop until he jolted. He locked onto my hair as I lowered completely down around him, controlling my reflex, then slowly releasing him from my clutch.

With tamed strokes, I rubbed him while taking a quick breather, then returned for one more taste while both hands pleasured him, as if I was grinding pepper. "I love you," he whispered indolently. I amplified my kisses for a few seconds more, then reduced to slow soft licks, triggering his body to slump over in elation.

I rose to face him, lifted my skirt, and sprung on top of him, screaming from painful delight. "Ih-Ih." I sighed, gripping onto the headrest.

He thrusted his dick upward, "You look so fucking beautiful tonight," he said, holding me in place just below my back.

I regained my composure and matched his rhythm, slow

deep strokes kneading my walls side to side. He reached for my face and I cradled his hand against my shoulder, while he ran his other hand down my back.

Escaping my hold, he placed both hands behind my shoulders and we locked eyes as he gripped them tightly. He stared at me with pure passion in his eyes and I grew weak. "I love you, too."

"Say it again," he begged.

"I love you."

"I loved you first."

His deep voice in its sultry state affected me uncontrollably. Harder and faster my hips grinded, while his hands spread my cheeks east and west. Sweat soaked between us, and our heat fogged the windows on the driver side of the car. "Ah!" Mash bellowed, holding me in place as I rested my head on his shoulder, savoring the moment.

Disheveled and gratified, I returned to my seat and the engine revved. Mash exhaled deeply. "Let's try this again. I need a smoke," he confessed, then drove us to the house.

We didn't speak for the twenty-minute ride, and I grew worried my forwardness was too much, too soon. I attempted to end the silent streak. "I'm going to hop in the shower."

"You know where the towels are," he said, and headed outside.

I watched him hit a joint sitting pensively by the pool, then left him there as I couldn't watch anymore.

I had showered, put on another one of his t-shirts, looked at my friend's pictures online, and nearly nodded off waiting for him to come to bed. An hour later he showered, and sat up scrolling through his phone, far away on his side.

As I waited for him to speak, I drove myself insane with worry. '*Say anything. Kill this silence please. What did I do to mess this up? He said he loved* **me** *for Christ's sake. Today was too perfect to end like this.'*

The past taught me not to react and be patient, so I did. I was confused and wanted to cry, but I refrained out of pride. My back remained facing him, but I could feel his eyes upon me.

"Nadia."

"Yes."

"About today..."

"It's okay. You don't have to..."

"I don't know what I'm going to do when you leave on Sunday," he said.

Shocked to hear him say such words, I turned around to face him, greeted by his solemn, handsome face. "What?"

"I've been thinking. Sunday is fast approaching and I don't want you to leave."

"You do realize you haven't said a word to me in over an hour, and I have been over here trying to figure out what I did to ruin this perfect day we shared."

"I didn't mean to make you feel uncomfortable. It wasn't my intent. I was just trying to come up with ways this could work for us."

"And."

"I just told you. I don't want you to leave. Today was one of the best days I've had in a long, long time."

"Me, too. How about we do as you said. Let's not think about Sunday." I slid next to him.

A simple slip of the tongue and expression of rage over an hour of silence could have ruined everything. His confession stunned me, more than his profession of love. He said it. I said it. But did we mean it? We were somewhere on the borderline of love and lust, and having been addicted to someone physically before, raised the question of did I truly know how I was feeling.

I fell fast, but I fell nonetheless. The past seventy-two hours felt surreal. Love was here, looking me in the face, showing me what it was like to have it in my grasp, and I didn't know what to do with it.

CHAPTER 5
HOSPITALITY

Travel began to wear on my body, and enigmatic pleasure added to my fatigue. Knowing he was concerned about a future with me eased my mind, and allowed me to relax in his home, and in his care.

I slept past midday, and probably would have slept longer if I had placed my phone on silent. Multiple phone calls back to back disturbed my rest. I had found a comfortable spot in the middle of the bed, and once you lose such a place there's no getting it back. I rolled over and checked my log, curious about the urgency of calls ringing nonstop. All of them belonging to Taylor.

I lied there with the phone in my hand, preparing myself for a conversation, I knew was going to be one-sided. I took a deep breath and returned her call, regretting it the moment I pressed connect.

"Hello Stranger," she answered.

I could hear rustling in the background, confirming she wasn't alone, and had placed me speaker. I took another deep breath, preparing myself for one of her performances. "Stranger?" I frowned.

"I haven't seen you since Saturday. We were supposed to be enjoying this trip together, and you have run off with some random white boy with your nose wide open. What's going on with you?"

"Whoa," I said, not happy with her word choice or tone. "Let's back this train up. I'm not with a boy, I'm with a man. You didn't see me before I left on Sunday, because we were all taking it easy."

"Nadia, you missed going to Paris."

"So what? I told you I preferred going to Ibiza over Paris remember? And going to Paris was optional. Why are you making a big deal about this? Do you need me for something?"

"I just can't believe you chose to be laid up with a guy you just met, instead of going to Paris with your girls."

"I wasn't laid up yesterday."

"Then do tell. What did you do?"

"I went to Spain."

Taylor scoffed and laughed in her wicked way, mumbling with the phone muffled by her hand. A commotion of noise ensued when I heard her faintly say in the background, "This bitch just said she went to Spain yesterday."

The voices of Khai, Shannon, and Isla became clear when Khai took over the conversation. "Nadia, everything is cool. What Taylor is failing to communicate, is she feels you have forgotten why we are here. But don't worry, I think it's just a bridal moment."

Taylor shouted from a distance, "I'm not having a bridal moment! She is supposed to be here!"

"Excuse me ladies," Mash interjected. "Taylor, I told Nadia I wanted to meet the bride and groom, so would you and your mate have dinner with us tonight at my house?"

"You should go," Khai whispered.

The line grew silent. I rolled my eyes at Mash, waiting for Taylor's theatrical performance.

"Sir, thank you for the very nice offer. Mash, is it?" she asked, knowing the answer to her question.

"Just say yes already. You know you want to." I interposed.

She huffed. "Well I guess my answer is yes then."

"I'll text you the address. See you at seven." The words swiftly left my mouth before I ended the call.

A POOL TABLE sat where a dinner table belonged. A highly critical and emotional guest was coming over, and dinner was to be served by my hands. With limited hours to prepare, the market run extended to multiple store runs, in search of foldout tables and chairs, a tablecloth, candles, vases, kitchenware and fresh flowers.

A pear and apple salad with a honey-lime vinaigrette chilled in the fridge, while my famous diced tomato short ribs, creamed potatoes, and sautéed spinach travelled through the house. For an added bonus, I baked Levi's favorite yellow cake topped with chocolate almond icing for dessert, and set it next to the floral centerpiece I arranged.

Taylor and Levi arrived on schedule. Mash welcomed them inside, and Taylor's eyes could not stop sizing him up. She became fixated with his hand around my waist, and hardly parted her lips, while Levi participated alone in the conversation. "Why are we still standing here?" I asked. "Let's get some drinks in those hands."

As we walked to the living room, Mash thanked them for bringing me to London. Levi was his normal modest self, cool and collected, and dismissed the notion they had anything to do with fate.

Taylor, on the other hand, replied, "You're welcome." I knew then we were in for a long night.

The men set off to smoke cigars in Mash's studio, while Taylor and I took a quick view of his house. Subtle sounds murmured behind me as she looked around each room, never offering a compliment.

When we made it to the kitchen, she stared at me as I carefully proportioned the dinner plates, smirking and shaking her head. "You seem right at home. Playing Suzy Homemaker," she chided.

"I made the apple and pear salad you like." I deflected.

"He seems to really like you." She continued.

"Taylor. I've never fell for someone this fast before."

"Fell? As in?"

"You know." I puckered my lips.

"You can't be serious." Taylor laughed. "You two are so—different."

"Have you seen how fine he is?"

"He's okay, but still. He's... and you're..."

"Yeah we are. And it doesn't matter. We click. I don't care about color. Only him as a person, and how he makes me feel. And he makes me feel damn good. I'm in love."

"Girl stop playing." She fanned me off.

"Judge me. Tease me. Do or say whatever you want. I've been bitten and I'm smitten."

"Okay calm down Foxy Brown. It's been what four days?" She rolled her eyes.

"I know it sounds crazy, but it's true."

"Do you love him like you loved Dylan?"

"Dylan who?"

Taylor stood with her mouth slightly parted, and a look of disbelief on her face. Mash and Levi's voices grew closer entering the temporary dining room, snapping Taylor out of her zone.

She surprised me and carried the salad to the table, and I trailed her with the dinner plates, enjoying the sounds of the men getting on so well.

I considered Levi one of my male best friends. He was always a delight, a great role model for the youth, patient, and respectable. Being the great conversationalist he is, he kept the table talk interesting with discussions of business, sports, books, politics of the west, and entertainment knowing it was Mash's field.

"If you don't mind me asking, how much does all of that equipment run you?" Levi asked.

"Quite a pretty penny. It's taken me years to get everything I needed for a fully functioning lab, but it was worth it. Studio time costs an arm and a leg. Now I can work from home and save my coins."

"You seem to be doing well for yourself— for a deejay," Taylor added.

"Babe, that's inappropriate." Levi scolded her.

"It's okay. I do more than deejay at clubs and spin records. I do sound engineering, sound mixing, radio guest spots, and produce music. My next project is producing the score for a movie coming out this winter."

"By score you mean add the music to the scenes, right?" Levi asked.

"Yes. It will be a major accomplishment for me."

"Have we heard any of the music you produced in the U.S?" Taylor asked.

"Probably not on the radio, but satellite radio spins them. Techno is bigger over here than it is in the States."

"It amazes me how different things are here. I can't get past the driving on the wrong side of the road," I said.

Levi, Mash and I laughed at my comment, while Taylor stewed at how great we were getting along.

Mash shared a look with Levi. "You'll get used to it."

Levi chuckled. "Nadia, you did good with this one."

I nodded and rubbed the back of his neck, avoiding eye contact with the opposition across the table. Taylor rejoined the conversation, and changed the subject to her wedding.

Mash didn't know Taylor well enough to know she was baiting him. Unaware of her trap, he thought it would be good to say something about the wedding to appease her. "Is it okay if I come to the wedding as Nadia's plus one?" he asked.

"Weddings are for people you are close with. You know family and friends, and we don't know you like that." She bitched.

"Don't listen to her man, of course you are welcome. Baby, the man has invited us into his home. Don't be rude." Levi reached for her hand.

"That's the second time you've chastised me tonight."

Levi and I put our forks down knowing where the night was headed. We had years of experience with Taylor's flip side. Her ugly head had arrived, looking for a fight, and wouldn't stop until she got one.

"Am I the only person here who realizes how crazy you two are being? Nadia, can you honestly say this isn't moving too fast?"

"I told you it was moving fast, and I'm on board. I'm happy."

"And you?" Taylor pointed her fork towards Mash. "Is this your first interracial relationship, Mash? What is your real name?"

"Wow. And no, it's not. My legal name is Maximus Sharper. Get is Ma, Sh, Mash for short."

She scoffed. "You live half a day apart— by plane at that, how serious can you be with my friend?"

I tapped Mash on the leg, and shook my head *no* to not answer her. Levi and I shared a look, then I faced Taylor. "Don't speak to him like that. He invited you here, and you're being beyond rude. What's up with you?"

Taylor was blown away I confronted her behavior. She huffed. "This is all insane to me. You two are acting like you're so in love. You know nothing about each other."

"I know enough, and I do love her," said Mash.

I lifted my head and shared a smile with him. He leaned over and kissed me gently, then looked to Taylor.

"And we don't owe anyone an explanation of what is happening between us."

She looked to Levi to speak on her behalf. "I'm not chastising you Tay, but baby he's right."

Taylor threw her hands up. "Apparently, it's 3 to 1, so I'll go back to minding my business. I've said what needed to be said."

I took a deep breath. "Let's agree to disagree here. Everything is cool. When you bit my head off earlier, I assumed you were feeling like I was stealing your thunder. I promise you that is not my intent. I'm here for you. We just want to spend as much time together as we can before I leave."

"Baby, apologize to them," said Levi.

"No need. I know she's stressed out about the wedding. We're cool." I patted her hand across the table.

"Well I'm glad we got that cleared up, because I think I found my first bromance," said Levi, pounding fists with Mash. "Now can we cut this cake?"

CHAPTER 6
SHOTS

Naked I lie in his arms, my eyes closed enjoying his caress against my back. My hands pressed against his firm chest, my head next to his. "Morning," he said.

My eyes greet him and I smile. "Five more minutes. Please." I begged.

"Then five more minutes it is."

The morning was opposite of the night prior. With friends we laughed, danced and drank ourselves into slumber, but woke to the realization our secluded days had come to an end. This day was inescapable. He walked me inside and we said our goodbyes at the elevator. I did a quick change into my purple Team Bride t-shirt, and I was back on duty, fulfilling Taylor's every wish and command.

London weather was fickle. Sunny with wicked winds, making it chilly and warm depending on the hour. The overcast and breezes didn't serve well for some of the planned family activities. During the downtime, we stood around and gossiped, half-assing around when it came time to pick up where we left off. The constant stop and go killed the competition, and purple versus green ended earlier than planned.

With lunch an hour away, improvisations were made as the family selected someone to sing a solo, forced the younger children to entertain, and fought one another for the microphone to speak about the wedding— the ones who weren't asked to be a part of the ceremony.

The caterers arrived and like good worker bees, the wedding party saw that everyone was seated and fed, before ourselves. The bridal party table was then allowed to clock out, and we gathered at our assigned table lastly, a few feet shy from the elderly section.

The memo hadn't been received to everyone, that Taylor was feeling a certain way about my absence, as her cousin Janine pried into my business. "Where have you been?" she asked.

"Around," I answered.

"I haven't seen you. I thought you were jetlagged or something when you didn't come with us to Paris."

"No, I wasn't jetlagged."

"She was in Spain," Isla blurted.

"I didn't know we had the option to choose where we wanted to go," said Janine.

"We didn't," said Isla. "Did you and Taylor work everything out?"

"Yeah. I think she had a good time last night."

"Oh, so there was drama." Janine inquired.

"No, there wasn't any drama, but since everything is cool now, I have to know. What is it like being with a white man?" Shannon asked.

"So, it was you they were all whispering about." Janine told.

"They were whispering about me?"

"It wasn't like that. When we went to Paris, Taylor was upset when she found out why you weren't there is all. They may have overheard a thing or two, but it's nothing to fret about," Khai added.

"Now that that's squared away. Give us the *deets*," said Shannon.

"My lips are sealed. And don't ask me anything about the past couple of days."

"Then tell us about the nights." Shannon joked. "Come on Nadia. You've been gone for like three days. If it was whack, you wouldn't have stayed over there so long. Now quit playing and give me something. You got down with the swirl, now tell your girl." Shannon squeezed my shoulders.

"Why do you think I fucked him?"

"Didn't you? Can you verify if London men are the worst lovers?"

"No comment." I turned up my nose.

"I know you did it. From now on Nadia, I'm calling you GK. Grandma Klump. *"That's the only white man make me moist!"* Shannon quoted in the voice of the famous character.

The entire table burst into laughter. Tears formed in my eyes as I cried laughing at her antics. An uncanny rendition of the scene from *The Nutty Professor* movie.

"Do not call me that!" I begged, wiping my eyes.

"He is a hottie. I know that much?" said Shannon.

"How do you know?"

"I looked him up online. Hell, everyone's met him except me."

"Pull up his picture. I want to see him, too," said Janine.

"Shannon did more than look up his picture," said Khai.

"He is a celebrity. They always put their personal information out there. What people make per movie, net worth etc...

You're in good hands." Shannon signaled the ok symbol with her fingers, then showed his picture to Janine.

"Oh yeah. I'd ride up to his house butt naked on a horse covered in honey." Janine joked.

Her comment led to more tears and crying laughter amongst us. A few of us gasped for air. The others searched for napkins to wipe their lids, and the elders at the table nearby all smiled at us. Isla remained indifferent.

"What is your problem?" Shannon asked Isla.

"Why do you think I have a problem?"

"Because that was funny, and you are over there all stoned face."

"It wasn't that funny." Isla frowned.

"Don't worry about her Shannon, her beef is with me. She called dibs on my guy, which is ridiculous."

"Is that why you've been starting shit? I've been peeping how you've been getting in Taylor's ear. Not cool," said Khai.

"Isla, how do you call dibs on a man? Please do tell," Shannon inquired.

Snickers filled the table as all eyes were upon Isla. "If you will excuse me." She removed herself.

Shannon began her line of questioning once more, asking for details of my sexual conquest, and the appearance of my lover's lumber. I refused to share the details, but she wouldn't take no for an answer. She began explaining why her curiosity was getting the best of her.

"I just want to know if white men look like black men down there. You know, like you can be with a light skinned dude, but his thing will be brown, or you can be with a dark-skinned dude, and his thing will be reddish brown, or..."

"We get the picture Shannon," said Khai, giggling with the rest of the table.

"Seriously, what color is it? Inquiring minds want to know."

"I would say hummus," said Janine.

"Hummus? Hummus tastes just like it sounds— Hum-Ass," said Shannon.

The table paused in silence for a moment. A mixture of chuckles from Shannon's pun, and images of Janine's description pictured in our heads. We all looked at each other, guilty and tickled. Several hmm's and huh's were expressed, and collectively we burst into loud cackles, creating a stir and landing the attention of Taylor.

She waltzed over with Isla at her side. "Y'all better not be over here laughing at me."

"Don't worry. We're not." Khai assured her.

"What's so funny?"

"Shannon," we all said.

"I promise I'm behaving," Shannon replied in defense.

The laughter wasn't as boisterous as before, but it continued, and Taylor begged to be in on the joke. Janine took it upon herself to speak up.

"I was being my delightful self, telling your friends a few stories and what not. You came over just in time. Tell us, who could be the vanilla in your sundae?"

"You do realize our grandmother is sitting right there." Taylor pointed.

"Your grandmother might have a story she wants to share," Shannon teased.

"If she doesn't, I do!" shouted the grandmother's sister.

Shannon and Taylor's great-aunt snapped their fingers at one another, then shared a head nod of solidarity.

"She knows what's up," said Shannon. "Now let's see if it runs in the family. Who is on your list?"

"Nick Jonas," Taylor whispered.

"Is he legal?" asked Isla.

"If he isn't he will be when I'm done with him."

"Yeah let's hurry up and get you married," said Khai.

"I'd do Brad Pitt," said Shannon.

"Did you see him in Snatch?" Janine asked.

"Hell yeah. The scene when they burned his mama's van is why he is on my list. Come to think of it. He was smoking in Mr. & Mrs. Smith, too. Since you've already dipped your toes in the clear ocean, would you do it again?" Shannon asked Janine.

"Most definitely. Seth motherfucking Rogen."

"I can see that." Shannon concurred.

"He's like a total package for me. Funny, cute, high as hell, cool, and a head full of curly hair. Hell to the yeah."

"I have always thought Thor looked like he packed a punch," said Khai.

"He was wearing a piece in Vacation. It was not real," said Shannon.

"How do you know?"

"I researched it."

"Well he's still my pick." Khai shoved Shannon.

"And a damn good one." We assented.

"Don't leave out Captain America either," Janine chimed in.

"Yeah, he's very seasoned," said Taylor. "What about you Isla?"

"I support black love. I've never given it much thought." She turned up her lips.

"You told me you would fuck Jon Snow!" Taylor blabbed.

"I told you that in confidence!"

"Like you would ever meet him." Taylor teased.

"Jon Snow and Daario Naharis." I cosigned.

"Which Daario?" Isla asked.

"The first one."

"Yes *Lawd*. That Daenerys is a lucky bitch."

"Who the hell are y'all talking about?" Shannon asked.

"It's a Game of Thrones thing." Our voices synchronized.

"Why are we talking about this again?" Taylor asked.

"You know why." Isla snarled.

Levi pulled Taylor away for what looked to be a serious chat. Hand gestures, pouting, and pleading appeared to be the theme of their conversation. She returned to the table, gave me a dirty look, then accused Mash of being a troublemaker. "Your little friend has invited Levi, and his groomsmen on a party bus with strippers."

"What's wrong with a night out of fun and bar crawling?" I asked.

"Call him and tell him to rescind his offer," she demanded.

Under severe scrutiny, I dialed him. *'Don't answer,'* I sang to myself. Heavy music blasted through the line. No greeting, just vibrating bass and chatter in the background.

"Sorry about that love. I wasn't at a stopping point. Is everything okay?" he asked.

I sighed. "I don't think so. Taylor would like to have a word with you."

Before I finished my thought, Taylor swiped my phone from my hands demanding answers.

"How many people can this bus hold? How well do you know these strippers? Who are these people coming with you?"

"It's a party bus. Quite a bit I imagine. And I'm bringing the artist I'm working with at the moment. Whom I need to get back to."

"Expect all of us tonight. We're crashing the party."

"Taylor, I didn't mean to cause any trouble. It's my way of helping him celebrate before the wedding."

"What time do we leave?" She insisted.

"7."

"We'll be ready. See you then."

She handed me my phone as I gave her a death stare. I apologized to Mash for interrupting his work, then ended the call. Shannon could no longer contain herself.

"So we're going out tonight?" She bounced in her seat.

"It looks that way," I answered, pacifying my anger internally. *'Stay calm. It's her wedding. Let her have this one.'*

Across the room I locked eyes with Levi, who was shaking his head in disappointment. I mouthed, *"Sorry,"* as a defeated look crossed his face. In unison we shrugged our shoulders, continuing to play along with the bridal tantrums and ridiculousness.

To avoid further conflict, I skipped hanging out with the others at the sauna. I hadn't had a moment to myself for days, so while Khai was busy taking advantage of the hotel amenities, I hung back in the room for some me time. I showered, threw on my pajamas, pulled out my tablet, and fell asleep before tapping a key.

Shortly before gathering in the lobby, Mash texted.

M: *Come upstairs to room 414.*

He greeted me wearing a towel around his waist, wet in some parts, seducing me with his smile. "You know we don't have time for this." I grinned, stripping him bare and running around the room from him. He begged for a quickie, but pleasure had to wait with everyone waiting on us downstairs.

The bus rolled into the lot, and a cloud of smoke floated from the doors as they bolted open. The recording artists sat in the rear, the strippers posed on the pole, and the party had already begun without us.

Acquaintances were made once the wheels were in motion. The men crowded the rear, and the women housed the front. Bottles of liquor, cigars and weed loosened up the stiff bunch I was with, with the help of the strippers forcing us to dance with them.

They showed us some of their moves, and we shared some of ours, then the music mix blended into our favorite song. All of the bridesmaids jumped up, bounced and shouted, "I get it how I live it!" Sending the bus into a frenzy and vibrating the floor.

Harv Legend, the artist from Mash's session earlier in the day, groped my legs as if he were entitled to them. I brushed his hands away, and made my way towards Mash blowing smoke with Levi sitting across from him.

Harv's eyes followed me, forcing Mash to signal *She's with me* with a hand gesture.

"Is this wifey you were speaking of?" Harv asked.

Mash nodded yes.

"Man's not foul." Harv held up his hands.

Playing it safe, I toned down the dancing. Partially because of the grope, but also the contact high I had from the ganja flowing freely. Between the weed, and the sexy smoldering way Mash looked when he lowered his bottom lip to the side to exhale, I was turned on.

I sat in his lap and kissed him zealously in front of everyone. "Don't do me like that after you denied me in the room," he said in my ear.

"You miss me huh."

"You look sexy tonight. I love seeing you so carefree like this. Reminds me of the night we met."

"You look handsome as always. Who taught you how to dress?" I flirted.

"I put my garms together."

"Your friend keeps looking at us." I side-eyed toward Harv Legend.

"He's fam. He's harmless. Forget about him. I'm more concerned with getting you out of these jeans you have painted on. I can't wait to get you home tonight."

"You mean the room?"

"Wherever you and I are together is home for me."

"Hmm," I said, squirming on him. "I just got a little wet."

"Naughty Nadia. I might have to bend you over in an alley somewhere. All of this teasing, I should warn you. There will be no love making tonight. *Capisce*? Do you think you can handle it?"

"I know I can handle it."

'I hope I can handle it.'

Bar one interrupted our provocative moment. The crew went inside, enjoyed a few rounds at the bar, and took over the mucky, minuscule dance floor, while Mash and I made out under a dart board in the corner. The way he felt pressed against me ignited a fire in my jeans. It reminded me of my high school days, when I allowed my first boyfriend to hunch on me for five minutes against the wall in the den. The only five minutes of alone time I ever had with him in my house, before he found a girlfriend who actually put out.

I forgot how hot this made me. The urges bursting like flames, and throbbing uncontrollably. *'I wish I could have him right here, right now.'*

"Posse out!" Levi shouted, and the crew scattered back to the bus.

"I hope this bar crawl goes by quickly," Mash whispered, pulling me from the brick wall.

I stepped on the bus and the girls pulled me away. Grilling me about how openly affectionate I had become. Harv sat next to Mash, and the bass in their voices carried along with the music. With my back to them, I overheard Harv ask, "How in the hell did you pull her?"

"I got lucky," Mash answered modestly.

"The bird is bad. She could have easily been mine if I saw her first."

"Maybe, but I saw her first and here we are."

"Don't switch. Man's not on the defense. Easy."

"We safe."

Their lingo was hard to follow as their slang was unlike ours. It was choppy, and proper, and confusing at times— primarily because of enunciation. Not understanding completely what was said, I politely gave Harv a tight-lipped smile when I sat in Mash's lap, in hopes he would be cool, and take an interest in someone else.

He got the memo and returned to his friends at the back of the bus. A short ride later we arrived at Bar 2.

Half of the bus went inside, while the other half continued to dance in the aisles, and on the poles. We stayed behind this time, contemplating the safety of a quickie in the alley behind the bar. The absurdity of it made us laugh, and so for the remainder of the night we agreed to distance ourselves.

Bars 3 and 4 were neighbors on the same block, far away in an area that resembled uptown back home. Bar 3 was cleaner than stop one. My boots didn't stick to the floor, and the wood on the bar shined.

A fuzzy navel on the rocks served me well, alongside lemon pepper wings and fries. The guys crowded Levi at the opposite end loudly chanting, "Cheers!" and other male repartee and obscenities while throwing back shots.

"Next!" yelled a groomsman.

One by one we trickled in the bar down the block. This being the final stop, the entire party huddled at the bar, and did shots on the count of three.

"It's a celebration!" Shannon shouted.

We surrounded the bride and groom with hugs and cheers, then took to the small dance floor, filling the place to capacity. The girls and I got wild on the dance floor, dancing dirty and singing loudly.

Mash's eyes were glued to me frolicking about, but I pretended not to notice, loving every minute of his attention. "Posse Out!" shouted one of the groomsmen, and for the last time, we reloaded the bus to end the night.

By the time we arrived at the Mandarin, smoke veiled the bus, and everyone was sloshed. Without any regard for other passengers in the elevator, Mash and I acted like sex crazed maniacs. Buttons were broken, jackets stripped. My hands up his shirt, and his down my blouse.

The ride was steamy and the heat didn't stop once we stumbled inside our suite. What remained of my top was torn as we made our way to the bed. My jeans were the only thing in our way from touching familiar skin. I was hard-pressed against the linens when Mash unzipped my boots, aggressively slid my jeans down my legs, and stared at me with a beguiled face.

Heavily, I breathed with anticipation when he reached down, and put my boots back on. He pulled me off of the bed and said in a masterful tone, "Dance for me." I took my time getting into a slow rhythm up against him, swaying in the silence, then untying his boots.

My finger pressed against his chest, and guided him to the chair next to the bar where I poured him a swig. I glided across the room and retrieved my phone from my jacket, selected the mood playlist and Paula Cole's 'Feeling Love' set the tone.

Rubbing my hands across every sensuous zone of my body, I teased him with slow movements, body rolls, and flexes. Giving him what he wanted. His own private show of me in red lace lingerie.

Playful taps to my cheeks and high kicks pointing my heels to the sky, I reeled him over to the bed, where I posed with my back arched and tossed my hair.

He grabbed a patch of it, lowered his face to mine, and kissed me roughly tasting of pure vodka. "Remember what I said earlier. There will be no love making tonight," he whispered in my ear, then flipped me over and spread my legs far and wide.

He sucked my vulva hard with my lace thongs still on, then suddenly destroyed them as they frayed in half. There was nothing gentle or soft about his kisses to my pussy. These were fast, wet licks with vigorous suction and cupping. I pulled his shirt off in the midst of him making a meal out of me, and placed it in my mouth to keep down my screams. He held my hands down at my side until he was ready to enter, and this time he wasn't gentle like our previous encounters.

"Uh," I gasped at his insertion as he moved forward toward me, tonguing me hard and restricting my hands above my head. He kept his word from before. This was a strict fucking and exploration of my walls. There was no remorse in his strokes. No regret in his poaching. No shame in the sounds he made.

My boots were now touching my hands above my head as he continuously pounded me into the bed. He removed his shirt from my mouth and kissed me a little softer this time, then whispered, "I want to hear you taking this dick."

He found pleasure in my moans and restraint. Suppressed beneath my inhibitor pummeling pure joy from my juice, I had no room to wriggle as I was locked in his clutch. Pinned together as one, I couldn't stop him if I tried, and I didn't want to. I was tipsy, tired, and taking it— most of all loving the thrashing he promised to deliver.

I screamed to the heavens, "Papi, Papi, Papi!"

He shuddered and opened fire. "I'm about to shoot to the moon!"

Neighing atop me, his hands clasped my neck with a mild squeeze, then he fell next to me. Winded. Breathless. Complete.

CHAPTER 7
GOODBYE

Underneath the loading zone we parted ways once more. Paris this time. He watched me walk through the revolving door, reveling in the damage he'd done hours before. He texted.

M:*I won't be like that always.*

N:*A good manhandling is alright every now and then.*

A full day of bride responsibilities began with a trip to the Shoreditch district for shopping, followed with wedding prep at the hotel spa. I was in no mood for hours of walking, and trying on clothes after the smashing I'd received, but to keep the peace I didn't stray from the schedule.

We returned to the hotel and gathered in the salon/spa for manicures, pedicures, and hair trials. Full service massages weren't a part of the package Taylor selected, but I was in need. My legs, feet, and back enjoyed a deep tissue massage, as I waited for my turn with the manicurist— charged to room 414.

With the entire bridal party present, the spa offered selections of Rosé, Pinot, and Champagne. We sipped while being pampered, then gave a toast to the bride for hosting a memorable getaway.

"If it weren't for you cousin, I would have never come to this place. But I'm glad I did. Being a bridesmaid is not my forte, but when you said it was a week-long event of fun out of the country, I said why not," Janine confessed.

"And thank God we don't have hideous dresses," said Shannon.

"I wouldn't do that to you guys."

"And last night! I haven't had that much fun in years." Janine celebrated.

"We did have a good time. Didn't we? Aren't you all glad we crashed the men's party?" Taylor took credit.

"Here, here. I was so messed up I hooked up with one of Levi's cousins," Shannon confessed.

"Which one?" Taylor asked.

"I can't remember his name. I'll point him out at rehearsal."

"That's a damn shame," said Khai.

"She's not the only one. Right Janine?" Miri, Janine's younger sister revealed.

"Stop telling my business."

"Which reminds me, does anyone here want to trade roommates, because mine brings home random men in the middle of the night," Miri chided.

"Who did you hook up with Janine?" Taylor asked.

"The rapper guy." Janine lowered her head.

"He was trying to get at everybody. Why did you let him hit?" asked Shannon.

"I was messed up. His team was doing a party pack in the back of the bus. I took a molly or ex and got serviced."

"They sounded like animals in the bathroom. I had to put a

pillow over my head. No one wants to hear their sister having sex." Miri complained.

"Okay from here on out. No one is to hook up with anyone else. Got it?" Taylor ordered, and we all snickered.

"General Tay, you can only babysit one punani. Yours," said Shannon, causing everyone including the service team to cry with laughter.

Nightfall quickly approached, and I made a second attempt to get some writing done. Avoiding the blank page, I read emails, sorted every item I purchased, and organized my luggage to make everything fit. *'2 days until I see him again, then back to reality.'*

Finally, I sat against the headboard, reflecting on the past few days. There was so much to journal, I didn't know where to begin, so I typed whatever came to me in flashes. The club, dancing, kiss, concert, kiss, romantic stroll, sex, the plane, the rock, the sunset, sex, sex, the dinner, the crawl, the make out session in the bar, and sex again.

I chuckled when I proofed my outline and saw how many times I wrote sex. Then I thought about it, about him, about how he made me feel, and how I missed him already.

Thirty minutes later, my journal had turned into a first chapter draft of the past week. *'There's no way I could go into detail about us,'* I thought and closed my computer.

I still felt him from last night. My hands crept in between my legs pressed together, holding myself in an attempt to savor the feeling. In a fetal position, I dozed off. Completely tapped and missed my paramour's call.

The ringing of the hotel phone woke me the day before the wedding. *This your wake-up call. Enjoy your day*, said the recorded voice.

One last hurdle before the main event, the rehearsal dinner. My assignment— oversee the decor.

The morning was spent catering to Taylor. Collectively, we had to see that she remained calm, verify the hotel staff arranged the decorations according to her wishes, iron her clothes if need be, and make her feel like royalty which was why she chose England for her destination wedding.

Levi's grooms relaxed while the bridesmaids ran around like chickens with their heads cut off. Happy hour began early for them, showing up glossy and red-eyed, giggly and frisky.

The vibe was stressful yet energetic, and I learned weddings were an emotional time, watching Taylor cry on and off until it became contagious. When we lined up she cried. When Isla and Drew, the best man, walked in the bride and groom's place, she cried, making Levi cry. Then Isla cried, creating a wave of tears in the party and family members.

Time ran over in the rehearsal as emotions ran high. The banquet manager saved the night, interrupting our last run to remind us of our dinner reservation.

The hour was late, but that didn't stop the drinks from flowing. Family and friends sang praises of the happy couple, taking turns as they saw fit, to stand and share special moments from their past, and wishing them well in their future. A toast was made to the bride and groom, then dinner was served.

Continuing from earlier, the drunken groom party became bold and flirtatious, working the room with hopes to get lucky. I excused myself while the others mingled to answer a call, and returned promptly to complete my list of duties for the night.

Unaware I was within listening distance, Isla had my name on her tongue, ridiculing my behavior to Janine and Taylor, who stood by and allowed the bashing. Anger was my first reaction, but it quickly faded as I reminded myself Isla was jealous and had every right to be. I waited a while before gracing them with my presence, and carried on as if I heard nothing, being a good friend and not ruining Taylor's moment.

With the wedding only a few hours away in the afternoon, I turned in early. I didn't disturb Mash since he was working, and out of boredom I wasted money, ordering a movie that ended up watching me, exhausted from the harrowing day.

BRAIDS DRAPED in the front of our hair, with loose wavy curls falling from the ends, the bridal party circled Taylor in her room, perfecting her strands and her straps, securing her fears from the unknown, and praying for a perfect day. The tears returned and her hands shook with nerves, delaying her glam team to have her ready on time.

Running fifteen minutes late, Levi stood outside of her room, and shared a moment with her. The last push she needed to get the show on the road.

One by one, we preceded her down the aisle in our mint colored gowns and fuchsia florals in hand. The ceremony began with a solo from a member of Levi's family, then a poem read by Taylor's aunt. The minister performed a lengthy service with a scripture reading, followed by a short story about the roles of a husband and the duties of a wife.

I searched the room for Mash, hoping to catch a glimpse of him since we barely spoke after he left. *'Where is he?'* I wondered, after scanning the crowd with no luck.

Taylor's waterworks returned during the lighting of the unity candle, and Levi wiped away her tears. The room including myself cried along with her, though mine were a mixture of happy and sad tears. I was moved by the love in the room, but sad the time with my love was ending.

Man and wife were pronounced, then cocktail hour entertained the guests as we posed for a million photographs on the hotel property. Watching the newlyweds love on each other made me grow antsy to get to the reception hall.

The celebration began, the wedding party introduced, and still no sign of Mash. The first couple dance ended. Taylor danced with her father, Levi with his mother and then mother-in-law, and the dance floor opened to everyone. It was then I realized. *'He's not coming.'*

It wasn't the way I would have said goodbye, but I understood the gift he was giving me. Our time would forever be cherished, I just wished I could feel his arms around me once more. If I had known our last kiss, would be our final kiss, I would have held it a while longer.

Listening to speeches and toasts and watching friends and family dance, I lost my composure. I needed to get to my phone, which was forbidden during the ceremony.

I slipped out of the reception and went up to our room, searching for something with his scent on it, but he had packed all of his belongings when he left for France. The only thing remaining in the room with his aroma was the pillow he slept on. I held it in my arms, imprinting the fragrance on my brain.

My phone had zero missed calls and one unopened text, not from him. I paced the room in disbelief. *'You did this to yourself.'* And I did. I let this happen. I lost control. I ignored my brain and listened to my heart. I was to blame.

A knock on the door disturbed me from my insanity. I ran to it with hopes I had worked myself up for nothing. Still no Mash. It was Khai. She had been watching me play pretend all day, and came to console my aching heart.

"Is everything okay?" she held my hand.

"I'm such a fool." I cried.

"You're far from a fool. What's going on?"

"The fairytale is over. He's not coming."

"What did he say?"

"Absolutely nothing. No call, no text, no show. And I get it. Why prolong the inevitable when he was already free from me ya know? Why leave Paris and come back here. He's not tied to me. He doesn't owe me anything."

"Sweetie, you're getting yourself all worked up. And for nothing I'm sure. He wouldn't just ditch you like that." She assured me.

"How do you know?"

"I saw you two together with my own eyes. He's crazy about you. Not to worry you, but maybe something happened. Like he missed his plane, or someone stole his phone so he couldn't call you. I'm sure he doesn't know your number by heart. No one knows anyone's number by heart. Calm down. Okay. If you haven't heard from him tonight, then worry. But right now, you need to come downstairs and enjoy yourself. Let's get you cleaned up."

She wiped my dripping mascara, and touched up the red areas on my face, concealing the emotional rollercoaster I was experiencing. We returned to the party, where I masked my true feelings by dancing with a persistent groomsman.

Once he became hard to shake, I faked a cramp and sat alone in the spectator chairs. Straight-faced and forlorn, occasionally faking a smile.

Simpering face Isla spotted me sitting alone. It was the moment she'd been waiting for all week. Tension ran down my spine just looking at her, but I had to be strong, and not let her belittle me, or get me riled up. *'Keep your cool. Don't let her see you like this. Don't give her the satisfaction.'* I preached to myself.

"Where is Mister 1s and 2s? I haven't seen him around for a few days. Trouble in paradise already?" Isla probed.

"Humph. Mister 1's and 2's. That's cute. How long did it take for you to come up with that one?"

"I'm just teasing. But for real though, where is he? I thought Taylor said he was your plus one?"

"You and Taylor have been doing a lot of talking about me and my plus one. Why is that?"

"What do you mean?" She stuttered, horribly hiding her guilt.

"I heard you last night. And I quote, "This weekend was supposed to be about you, and Nadia's been running around town with her nose wide open over a fling. She's in la la land." End quote. Sound familiar?"

"Did you seriously think it was something more? You're smarter than that."

"Isla, humor me. If he chose you that night, what would you have done?"

"Don't deflect. I was simply saying it was embarrassing how you were carrying on. But seeing as though he isn't here, I'm sure you've snapped back into reality. Sorry it didn't work out the way you wanted." She smirked.

"Now look who's deflecting. You didn't answer my question."

"You didn't answer mine. Do you know what your problem is Nadia?"

"Her problem is she isn't dancing with me," Mash interrupted.

Reaching for my hand in a tailored tan suit accentuating his broad shoulders, and a powder blue oxford shirt, he rescued me from Satan's daughter. I rose to my feet, coyly smiling with my head down, elated he was in front of me.

He escorted me to the dance floor and I gleefully followed his lead. "Do you know what you're doing captain. This is a fast song." I teased.

"Let's pretend it's a slow one," he said, holding me close. "You look amazing by the way."

"You clean up well yourself. Very dapper look you got going on here."

"Have you been crying?" he asked, kissing my neck.

"I had a slight meltdown, but I'm okay now."

"Why? What happened?"

"I didn't think I was going to see you again."

He held me from the nape of my neck, and placed his head against my mine, "I'm sorry I'm so late. I would never do something like that to you. I had a few errands to run before leaving Paris. One was finding these guys a wedding gift. Then of course, I had to get you something. I had to fight traffic, rush home to get dressed, get back in traffic, and now I'm here."

"Like I said before, I overanalyze everything. I thought you were making a clean break from me without all the drama."

"Look at me," he demanded, holding my chin up. "I told you I love you the other night. I mean what I say, and I say what I mean. Never forget that."

"I love you, too."

"I would have called, but you told me you wouldn't have your phone at the wedding. I got here as fast as I could. You have no idea how gutted I've been these past two days. I've done nothing but dread tomorrow. I want you to stay."

The thought had crossed my mind, but it was wishful thinking. I didn't dare tell him that. Instead I replied, "I wish I could."

"Tell me why you can't."

"You know why. My life is across the ocean."

"You can write from anywhere. I want you here with me. Let me show you the world. I've thought this through and I know it can work." He pulled me in closer.

"You're serious, aren't you?" My brows furrowed.

"Promise me you'll think about it." He sighed in my ear.

"I promise."

I inhaled his scent as we continued to dance, wrapped in one another's arms, slow dragging to the fast song playing, and the slow one after that. The dance floor was cleared to witness the bride and groom cut the cake. Levi and Mash shared a congratulatory embrace, and got on as they did earlier in the week. He placed an envelope in Levi's hand. "This is from the both of us."

We joined everyone at the banquet room doors, throwing lavender and dried flowers at the wedded couple, glowing upon their exit. To speed up the bridal party duties, both the maids and grooms delivered the gifts to Taylor's parent's suite.

Mash and I disappeared to our room filled with a range of emotions. We lied in bed laughing at the tele, snuggled close with sporadic moments of passionate lip exchanges. He wiped my tears when they fell, gazed at me in silence, and avoided eye contact with me when I added items to my luggage.

He stared at the floor from the edge of the bed in the middle of the night. I crept behind him, contemplating his request to abandon my life across the ocean. While kissing and squeezing his shoulders, I listened to him sigh, studying the brooding brows above his distant eyes in the mirror wanting to shout, "Of course I'll stay with you," but I was afraid. Afraid to be alone in London without my friends and family nearby as a safety net. Afraid he was who I had been searching for and I would mess it up. Afraid to take a chance.

"This is going to sound weird, but may I have the t-shirt you wore tonight?" I asked.

He removed my arms from around him, folded it neatly, and placed it in my bag. He sat in the chair near the mini bar, and poured himself a shot. "Leave me something of yours as well."

"Like what?"

"Whatever you want me to have." He avoided eye contact with me.

"Can we at least discuss how and when we are going to see each other again?" I huffed.

"I'll send you my schedule. You pick which city you want to come to, and I'll fly you in."

"What about you coming to see me?"

"I'll come when you tell me to."

"Are we okay?"

"Yeah. I just hate this day has finally come."

He threw his head back and gulped the harsh brown. I minced to the bar and stood in front of him, stroking his hair while pressing his head against my stomach. He looked up at me and told me he missed me already, kissing the back of my hand while rubbing on the back of my thighs. I hadn't felt his touch in two days, and my legs withered at his fingertips. It was time. He knew it. I knew it. We had become addicted to one another. Sexually. Wholeheartedly.

He grazed my nipples with his teeth. Toying with them, forcing the nerves in my drip to pulse. My bosom saluted him, pointing at the tip with each nip. I stood in front of him, holding on to his shoulders with a confounded mind, wondering what was this hold he had on me, but also how was I going to get along back home with him.

Seductive kisses began to melt against my skin. His approach was tender this time. Delicate strokes brushed up and down my back. Elongated kisses upon my neck. Now standing, he danced with me in circles around the small space beside the bar, then carried me to the bed.

His fingers drew lines from my feet, all the way up my legs as if he were making a mental image of them to keep. Then he kissed the exterior of my orifice with a closed mouth. Not once.

Not twice. Several slow and gentle pecks, observing the shocks in between.

'*Was this our last time together,*' I wondered.

I squirmed as I wanted him inside of me, but he made me wait for him. His tongue licked me everywhere it could reach, Frenching my lower lips as if it had a tongue of its own. I groused with my hands running through his hair. Sighing for him to ease the pain of my departure. And then he hovered over me. Waiting to give me what I craved.

Lingered atop of my desperate begging body, he looked into my eyes and rubbed his thumbs across my cheeks, then traced the outline of my bitten lips with his index finger.

I grew weak from the impeding attention being given to me. "Put it in," I begged. He refused. He wasn't done studying me. I pled again. "Mash, please let me feel you inside me." He wouldn't budge. He was in control, showing me what I would miss if I left.

And so, I lie there patiently beneath him, gazing into his eyes and brushing his face against mine, going mad from depravation, bracing for his vast entrance. "Unh," I whimpered from gratification the torture was over.

He grinned as if he was looking forward to hearing the sound leave my mouth. Back and forth we moved in unison, looking away deep into each other's eyes. "Stay," he said. I looked away. "Stay," he repeated, resting his head on my shoulder.

I gasped in between jabs, never responding to his request, losing the battle of holding back my tears.

My grind from below excited him. He wrapped my legs around his waist, moaning insatiably from the build-up. My ass encompassed his pressing palms, bringing me up further as he drilled for my black gold.

"Let me hear you say my name one last time," he ordered.

"Maximus," I moaned.

"Again."

"It's not the last time."

"Again."

"Maximus," I cried.

"I love you."

The climax was bittersweet. I hadn't felt so good and so bad at the same time ever in life. I was riddled with guilt, and without explanation, but mainly perplexed at his word choice. *One Last Time.*

Distance doesn't work well for most relationships, and I took his words to mean he was giving up before we started. I listened to him drift off, then slithered from underneath his arm. So much was on my mind I couldn't sleep. I texted Khai.

N:*You up?*

K:*I am now.*

N:*Can I come down? Please?*

K:*Sure thing.*

Khai placed the bolt lock outside of the door to keep it open for me, and sat propped up on the bed looking at me with her-*this better be good*-face. I sat at the foot of the bed and spilled my guts. "You know how you've always been there for me?"

"Yeah." Her voice dragged.

"I don't know what I would do if I didn't have you in my life."

"If this is about Taylor and Isla being shady to you, don't sweat it. We're friends, but sometimes friends get jealous of one another. It'll blow over."

"Maybe. But you know how the two of them have their thing, and you and I have our thing, and all four of us have Shannon?"

"Yeah, that's true."

"He asked me to stay Khai. I won't have you to run to if I do."

"Stay as in move here?" Her voice heightened.

"I guess. I haven't asked him to go into detail about it. He just keeps repeating stay, stay, stay."

"Do you want to?" Khai sneered.

"I have no fucking clue what I want! I wanted a good man. I found him. A gotdamn diamond in the rough to be exact. I've wanted someone to love me. And not just say it. But show it. And he does that. But why does he have to live on the other side of the world? If I stay, I'm giving up my world— for a man...That's sounds so bizarre don't you think?"

"It is a hard one. Especially this day and age when we are all talking about women's rights, and the fight for equality."

"And here I am considering doing something as bonkers as staying in another country for a man."

"But he's a good man." Khai's brows raised.

"Is he? We've known him for seven days. No, no, no I can't stay. My mother would kill me. I'd lose my best friend. I'd be over here all alone. Just forget I even came down here and bothered you."

I stood to leave, then sat back down in confusion. Silence sat between us as Khai stared at me half smiling, and half laughing at the back of her throat.

"Nadia, did you come down here so I could tell you what to do?"

"Maybe. No. I don't know. Probably."

"Well I can't make this decision for you. But I will say, you should clarify what he means by stay. Maybe he wants you to stay for a few extra days. That wouldn't be so bad. Ask him."

"A few days wouldn't be a problem."

"Exactly, but you have to have the conversation."

"And what if he means a few weeks?"

"Then you need to decide if he's worth you giving him that kind of time and attention. What are you afraid of?"

"That this will end like it did with Dylan. Being used and betrayed and thrown away like a piece of trash. That if I stay, he'll get bored with me and ship me home when he's ready, and I will have lost all of my respect." I wiped away my tears before they fell.

"This one is nothing like Dylan. I've seen how Vanilla Ice looks at you. And you him." She joked.

My mouth fell open, and my tears fell as a hard laugh echoed from my stomach. Trying to catch my breath I uttered, "Don't make me laugh." But we both fell over guffawing.

Moments later we simmered down, and Khai alerted me. "Everyone saw how he looks at you. I bet you didn't know all eyes were on you two when you were dancing. And I saw his face when he showed up tonight."

"He said he loves me."

"And I believe he does."

"I said it, too."

"I knew it!" She jumped up from the bed and clapped her hands.

"You think I'm crazy, don't you?"

"I think you're scared more than anything. Look, if you stay, you won't lose me girl. Hell, your man is rich he can fly me back and forth. By the way. Before you go I need to remind you, you owe me something."

"What?"

"The 411. Is it good girl?"

"Do all donkeys have a cross on their back?" I sashayed away and grinned at Khai's hands muffling her open mouth.

Mash was in the same spot I left him in. I crawled next to him and kissed his arm, his face, his shoulder and his neck while watching him sleep. I put my foot under his shin and stared at the clock, waiting for the alarm to sound. Eventually, the night got the best of me and I woke to a ringing telephone, and a fully dressed Mr. Sharper.

The room was silent, filled with tension and sadness. The housekeeping carts squeaked as they were pushed from room to room near our door, and became the topic at hand. "They begin early, don't they," I said. He glanced in my direction with half an impish grin.

I threw on the sweat suit I arrived in, and zipped up my final bag. Mash gathered the load with me close behind, and the click on the door triggered him. He stopped before making it to the elevator, held my hand, then offered to drive me to the airport. "That won't be necessary, but thank you," I declined.

Our fingers entangled on the ride down until we reached the lobby floor. Mash settled the bill while I stood with the other passengers waiting to board the shuttle. I encouraged the others to go ahead of me, waiting for my girls and Mash with my bags.

My hands began shaking as I stood on the curb, then I felt his hands cover mine from behind. He wrapped me in his arms one final time and felt my body quivering.

"You okay?" he asked.

I nodded yes, lying as best I could.

"Stay with me," he said, as the girls handed their luggage to the attendant.

"It was nice meeting you Mash," said Khai.

"Nice meeting you, too. All of you. Hopefully we'll get to hang out again soon."

I trembled. *'This is the moment I dreaded.'*

"And thank you for taking us on the bar crawl. When you come to the States we'll treat you right." Shannon shook his hand.

"I'm going to hold you to that." Mash forced a smile.

Khai looked me up and down, and then in the eyes. She placed her arms around me, and I dropped a tear, visibly shaking in front of everyone. She squeezed my shoulders, then said to Mash, "You take care of our girl now." Shannon turned around and questioned me with her eyes.

"Take care of our girl?" she mouthed.

I widened my eyes and handed my keys to Khai. "I'll call you if I need you. Love you and be safe."

Shannon's mouth dropped. She put her arms around Khai and I, and we hugged like teens going off to college. The driver split us up, calling for the last round of passengers. I watch them board the shuttle, shaking in my boots, second guessing my decision as the bus pulled out of the lot.

Mash swung me around and plastered his lips on mine with an audience watching. "Are you ready to take me home?" I asked.

He gloated. "You have no idea."

Tapping on the coated glass and making heart symbols with their hands, my friends shouted *love you* nonstop, as the shuttle engine throttled. We watched them fade in the distance, then loaded my bags in the car. "To the outskirts we go," I said.

My heart pounded, and my arms turned slightly damp of nervousness. I felt brave about my choice, and excited to be adventurous for the first time. I was living on a prayer, and taking a chance with my heart. Knowing the risk was high, and stepping out of my own way, certain I had found something profound.

I opened up a part of myself that was closed off, eager to explore a new chapter.

CHAPTER 8
PASSPORT

S tay. The one syllable word needed clarification. A few extra days to enjoy each other's company seemed ideal, but I avoided initiating the conversation, in fear it would ruin the vibe between us.

Our chemistry was unmatched. We weren't finishing each other's sentences or anything like that, but we were in sync. He made me feel welcome in his house, persisting I call it home.

Whenever he saw me working, he gave me space and room to breathe, or when he'd be gone all day to work on one of his various projects, he made sure I had access to money and one of his vehicles. And that was just the first week.

His level of consideration wooed me so, I dreaded the uncomfortable exchange we needed to have. Creating a genial atmosphere, I set up the folding table and chairs in the middle of the kitchen floor, and cooked one of my best meals, setting the mood for the discussion. As always, he greets me with a kiss the moment he arrives home. His hand finds the same spot between my waist and my back, and no matter what kind of day he's had, he lets me know he is happy to see me.

I tell him dinner is ready and to meet in the kitchen. We sit and chat for a bit, then casually I mentioned, "I looked up flights today, and I need to book something weeks in advance for a good rate."

"The rate doesn't matter. I'll cover it. What date are you looking to fly?" he asked, adjusting his frames.

"I was hoping we could discuss that. When do you want me to leave?"

'God I love him in those glasses.'

"Why would I want that?" His voice lowered as he stared me down.

"What did you mean when you asked me to stay? A few days? I've been here over a week."

"Honestly, when I asked, I didn't have an end date in mind." He hypnotized me with his gaze.

"I don't want to outstay my welcome is all."

"You still don't get it, do you?" His lips parted.

"I think I'm starting to."

'That's a come-hither look.'

We lunged across the flimsy table and burned from the passionate fire between us. The cheap table surprisingly held up against our quick stint of fucking in the middle of the meal.

This had become my new normal. A simple look, or accidental graze against my skin ended with my legs in the air, or me bent over the couch.

I had no idea when I was going home, and the time had come for me to face my mother with an answer to that very question. By the end of week two I was in Paris, following my lover around in the city of lights, narrow streets, delectable pastries, and historic museums.

I took photographs of old dated buildings, and attempted to converse with the staff of the hotel in their language—

desperately I tried to remember what I learned back in high school. The fashions of the women walking the streets were all awe-inspiring, but the highlight for me were the indulgent chocolate croissants.

Mash served as a tour guide showing me the normal attractions, and hidden gems people like himself only knew about. His access to places was notable, and during this trip I learned how important he was. I was blinded by his kindness and attention in the beginning, overlooking how the world viewed him and his work. Quickly, I became acclimated to the world of fame.

Sitting out on sound check, I laid back in the penthouse suite his promoters provided, and overlooked the city. The Eiffel Tower glittered over its admirers, and the streets were buzzing. The owner of a café across the street, swept the side-walk just before turning her signage to *fermee*.

Moments later she locked its doors, and set off holding the hand of whom I assumed was her daughter. I watched them until they turned the corner, exhaled a few times, and dialed my mother.

"Your grandmother and I had a nice chat about you little girl," she answered.

"Good things I hope. How is she? How are you?"

"I'm my usual self, but your grandmother is not. She said you haven't called her in weeks. You normally call her every day."

"She's right. I haven't been myself lately."

"Oh, we know." My mother scoffed.

"Is she mad? Are you?"

"Truthfully, as long as you are safe, we are fine with what-ever it is you are doing. What exactly are you doing? Besides laying up with a strange man. And spare me the details."

"I'm writing. And traveling. I'm in Paris right now. It's beautiful Ma. We should have done things like this. You know?"

"Traveling wasn't our thing. I'm glad you're doing it though. Is your friend with you?"

"Not at the moment."

"Well tell him as long as he doesn't hurt you, he won't have anything to worry about. Your friends have given me his address, so I know how to find him."

"I'm in good hands Ma."

"Seems so."

"I just wanted to tell you that, and tell you I miss you, and I'll see you soon. I love you."

"I love you, too, baby."

Weight lifted from my shoulders. I mistakenly thought that was going to be the hardest phone call of my life. I expected to be chewed out for my reckless behavior and rash decisions, and was grateful I received understanding and support instead. Then I remembered, I had to call my favorite person in the world, Grams, who was sure to cut me with her sharp tongue.

The car returned to chauffeur me to the concert. On my way out of the lobby, I stopped at the postal stand and wrote Grams a few lines. *'This should buy me some time before my lashing,'* I thought, before leaving it with the concierge.

Nightlife in the city reminded me of the years I spent in college. Seeing the crowds of women laugh amongst themselves, and having a good time, made me wish my friends were sharing this experience with me. *'I missed that opportunity, but it was so worth it.'*

For a brief moment, I became sad. I understood how it looked when I bailed on them to go to Spain. It came across as selfish, but I was sure they would have done the same thing if they were in my shoes.

As I passed several groups of women, I began to miss them, and wondered what they were doing back home. Then I remembered it was bowling night, and I wasn't missing anything except shit talking in a smoke-filled alley wearing borrowed shoes— having a good time nonetheless.

Backstage was reminiscent of Taylor's wedding day. Stressful, fast paced, lively, and crowded. A stage hand escorted me to the dressing room tucked away in a dark corner. It could have used a major facelift, cleaning, painting, or demolishing, but as I sat and looked around, I understood why it looked like a pit stop. It was. Acts from all over signed the walls, dressers, and chairs. It was the image of filthy history, and for entertainers a rite of passage.

The clamoring of the crowd amplified the artists as each went on. I stood stage right with the other VIP pass owners, watching Mash and the artists perform.

Unlike his gig at the tent, this crowd was massive and electrifying, and by the end of the show had made their way backstage somehow to meet the acts. It was unsettling to watch woman after woman throw themselves at the artists. I stood far away in a dimly lit shadow of a boulder taking it all in.

Fuming in jealousy with flashbacks of deceit. Mash was humble and acknowledged all those who approached him, which was a great look for him. I, on the other hand, had been given a front row seat to a world I was sure my insecurities couldn't handle.

The stage hand found me in the corner, and escorted me to the car down a hallway to a tunnel, where the artists come and go. I sat there for nearly thirty minutes waiting for Mash to come out, and when he finally did he looked beat.

"All done," I asked.

"That was insane at the end. Where were you?"

"I got lost in the crowd, so I stepped back to give the fans their space."

"Did you enjoy the show?"

"I was blown away. I must admit. I didn't know you were this big of a deal. Seeing it firsthand is different from reading tabloids."

"Stop." He covered his face and blushed.

I could have and should have let it end there, but doing what I normally do, I continued to reach. "How do you handle all of the fans coming at you like that?"

"What are you getting at?" he answered my question with a question. "I feel like there's more to that question."

"Humph. I'm not too keen on seeing women put their hands all over you." I regretfully admitted.

"Imagine being the person who doesn't enjoy people putting their hands all over you. It sucks, but it comes with the territory of what I do."

"I didn't think of it that way." I bit my lip.

"Well, you're about to see more of it. I just got an updated schedule, and we'll be hitting the road pretty heavy over the next few weeks, so get ready."

'We? Next few weeks?'

As Mash prepared for his crammed schedule, he spent hours away from the house rehearsing with the acts for the upcoming shows. I made an effort to keep myself busy by enrolling in exercise and dance classes, and people watching at cafes for writing inspiration.

The house was peaceful with Mash gone most of the day, and the quiet time allowed me to mentally decompress and write diligently. Submissions about travel, western news from an eastern perspective, and romance excerpts kept me occupied the many hours I was alone.

When boredom struck, I revisited the non-fiction story I began writing at the Mandarin, adding bits and pieces to it, giving myself a few shameful giggles.

Shy of a month, the hectic schedule began with the first stop in Cannes for a film festival. Mash had been hired to work a few parties, and as requested gifted me with passes to screenwriting workshops and seminars. It felt good to do something of my own interest, and not exist as the travel companion following him around all day.

I was on my own in the streets, sight-seeing and taste-tasting when the seminars ended. Basking in the sun on the beach, taking full advantage of my me time.

As Mash's schedule opened up, we won and lost money in one of the casinos, before sailing on a private yacht with one of his industry associates.

Snooty and elite minded people lounged on the vessel. Models in bathing suits, champagne every few feet, and A-list actors and actresses acting holier than thou.

My insecurity went into overdrive every time a famous woman tugged on Mash's arm, or tapped him on the shoulder, overly smiling in his face. I didn't think I would ever get used to feeling inferior to powerful women. *'How do I measure up,'* constantly crossed my mind in the presence of these people. They were desired beings making their own money, compared to me the penniless shadow.

The boat docked near our resort, so we strolled through the villas taking in the night air. Mash asked about the seminars I attended as an icebreaker, then questioned my behavior on the boat. "Talk to me."

"About what?"

"Earlier tonight? I noticed you shut down. What caused that?" He paused his steps.

"Just wasn't my crowd." I pulled him along.

"Is that all?"

"Yep."

He knew I was lying. He could feel something was wrong, but he didn't pressure me to say. He took me by the hand and respected my moment of withdrawal, though my silence rattled him. *'Lack of confidence is a turnoff,'* I said to myself, wrapping my fingers around his. "I'm fine." I assured him, knowing eventually I would be.

The next morning, we flew to Amsterdam. Two days in the city didn't give us time to explore the way I had hoped. Amid the rumors of it being well known for its red-light district, I wasn't interested in seeing sex-trafficked women work. I preferred to visit the museums, and taste the world-famous crepes as research for a travel submission, but time didn't allow it. Neither did the congestion of the city. I bust my ass riding a bike as the streets were overly crowded, and spent my short time taking it easy in the room.

Before leaving the Netherlands, I mailed post cards to my mom and Grams, filling them in on my travels, then it was wheels up. Four days until the next show I had no interest in attending.

After taking a day to recuperate from Cannes and Amsterdam, I began looking at flights again. I was homesick. I was tired. And I was losing myself in someone else's world. His world was exciting nonetheless, but my receiving rejection letter after rejection letter murdered my sense of self. My mind constantly wondered, *'What am I doing with my life.'* I needed to regroup.

Without discussing it with Mash, I booked a flight on the night he was due in Barcelona. I had three days to tell him, but couldn't muster the courage. Nor was there ever a good time to do so, being that he was exhausted when he made it home.

Every night he greeted me with a kiss, showered, ate, and laid under me while I keyed my soul away, still attempting to prove I was worthy of my craft. With nothing to lose, I submitted a synopsis of my Mandarin piece, to a production company in search of material to produce, then woke Mash to tell him I was leaving.

A light stroke to his shoulder led him to twist. Delicately, I massaged his shoulders to wake him. He grunted and mumbled for a few seconds, eventually opening his eyes. "Something's up," he muttered.

"I have to tell you something."

"It must be bad news."

"I'm homesick." I confessed.

"This again."

"I booked a flight."

His eyes widened as he lifted and leaned back against the headboard. He looked straight ahead, avoiding eye contact with me. "I kind of felt you were getting sick of me with the late nights and the shows, but I didn't think it was this bad."

"I'm not sick of you. I just need to go home. For a little while. I was thinking maybe you could come see me when your schedule opens up."

"What will you do when you get there?"

"For starters, check on my mother. Check on my house. Maybe drive down to visit my Grams."

"And then what?"

"What is with your tone?"

"I'm not understanding what is going so wrong here, that you are rushing to go back home."

"My life dammit! I just told you I was homesick. I never said anything was going wrong here. I just need to be around my people. Be around my things. Not feel like a kept woman or a shadow puppet. Hell, I'm practically a citizen."

He turned towards me but said nothing. He was looking through me and I couldn't take it. I couldn't take him or the silence. I left the bed and continued to rant. "Do you know I haven't had one article published since I've been here? I feel like I'm losing myself."

"I didn't know you were feeling that way. You never said."

"You never asked. You just keep putting off the discussion of when we would go to the States together."

"Nadia, if you had left after the wedding, I would have visited you by now."

"I'm not so sure you would," I said, pacing the room.

"I would have. But you stayed, and I thought if I played my cards right, you would never want to leave. It never occurred to me you would get homesick."

"You have done everything right. I love being here with you. I'm just..."

As I paused, he followed me to the window. I looked into the darkness, searching for the words to end my sentence. He placed his chin atop my shoulder and wrapped his hands around my waist. "Do I make you happy?"

"Very much so," I said, leaning my head against his.

"Then what can I do to remove this scowl from your pretty face?" he asked, stroking my cheek.

"Maybe take some time off and come home with me."

"I give you my word, we'll set a date. I'll have some things moved around tomorrow, then we'll go from there. Cool?"

"Un huh."

"I planned something special for us this weekend. Say you're still coming with me."

"Have I ever let you down?"

"Not once." He turned my face towards him and kissed my lips. "So this is what it's like to argue with you huh?"

I blushed and placed my arms around him. "That was not an argument. More like a disagreement."

"I don't know— you got a little feisty a second ago."

"You call that feisty?"

He grinned. "It kind of turned me on. Do you need help getting the rest of it out of you?"

"Oh no. I have work to do."

"So do I." He picked me up and carried me to the bed.

'*Why can't I say no to this man?*'

In the morning, I cancelled my flight home and packed for Barcelona, curious about these special plans he spoke of.

Once again, my feet touched the soil of Spain. Its colored beauty could not be ignored from the sky, but to see the murals and buildings up close were breathtaking. My host knew the ins and outs and kept me on guard for pickpockets, while we roamed the city exploring the streets and museums.

The next day was an early one, as Mash wanted to show me more of the city before reporting to sound check. We took a brief stroll in the Gothic Quarter. Narrow lanes and eerie architecture eventually led us into a shopping market, with novelty and keepsake items targeted for tourists.

My eyes locked in on a kiosk selling handmade rings, made from wire and beads. The intertwining of a black and blue band spoke to me, and with permission the attendant allowed me to slip it on my finger.

My face expressed I liked the piece before I could verbally say so, and without asking, Mash purchased it. He then asked the artist to take his measurements, and make him one to match mine.

With an hour to kill before picking up the order, we ate

street food, sat and listened to a band, followed a map of the well-known historic churches, then returned to the market.

The craftsman earned a healthy tip, by crafting matching bracelets with the identical pattern of the rings. I couldn't stop admiring my matching set. It reminded me of the hand-crafted jewelry sold downtown on the market in Charleston.

I stuck my hand out and dangled my wrist side to side at least a dozen times, fascinated at how the colors moved and shined in the sunlight.

"You love it that much?" Mash teased.

"I do. I respect the work of creative people, and I love to support artists. I know it's only wire and beads, but working with beads requires talent."

"You can have my bracelet. One for each arm."

"Thank you. I'll take it."

"One more thing. Marry me tomorrow."

"Don't play." I smirked at him.

"I'm serious. It's the only reason I wanted the ring."

"I thought you just wanted to match mine."

"Yes. As husband and wife."

"My feisty side didn't scare you away?"

"I've had this on my mind for a while now. I had this whole thing planned out for when we went home, but I don't want to wait. Let's do it here."

The look on his face exposed his truth, as he gazed at me with love in his eyes. "Tell me the worst thing about you," I said.

"I'm jealous." He confessed.

"So am I."

"I've seen enough to know I will weather any storm with you. Say you'll be my wife. Say you'll marry me."

The concierge in our hotel located a priest to perform the ceremony on the beach. I bought an inexpensive white sundress in the village, and tied white flowers around the thread in the hotel sewing kit. Pinning it into my hair, I walked barefoot on the beach, admiring my soulmate in his white t-shirt and slacks.

The wind and the mist blew my straight hair curly, while the sun blessed its light for those spectating to see. Hand in hand, we eloped. No big show. No drama. Just he and I, vowing to love each other forever.

CHAPTER 9
MRS

I smiled to myself for most of the flight home. Thinking about the way my husband couldn't have picked a better moment, a better place to ask me to be his wife.

My face was flushed, looking down at the stillness of the ocean beneath me. Giggling to myself as I reminisced about our consummation. The flickering candles. The calla lilies thrown all over the floor. The tenderness he displayed the moment I undressed when we returned to the room. The wind against my breast, the second time we made love on the balcony. The beast he became outside slaying me against the glass door.

We were rabbits before, so I didn't know what to call us now. Jack rabbits maybe? Whatever the species, we were animalistic with each other. I couldn't get enough of him. And now, his home was truly my home. Our home. The way that sounded put a bandage on my being homesick for a while.

Instead of searching for flights to America, I was scheduling when and where we would honeymoon, researching dual citizenship, and contemplating how to break the news to my mother. To my friends.

The response from the embassy took days, and the information we needed turned out to be complicated. I had to prove I was living with Mr. Sharper for over a week, then we could apply for a license in 21 days to make our union legal. I would also have to apply for a visa. The only visa I was ever interested in was the kind that swipes.

My first time travelling out of the States, led me to see parts of the world I never imagined I would visit, and changed my life. I no longer felt I was losing myself. I finally understood I was gaining a partner. The person I had been looking for.

Mash's tight schedule allowed us four days to honeymoon. Giving me total control, I chose Italy. It was the only place I could get the perfect wedding gift— The best pizza in the world, and meet my mother-in-law.

Valeria was stunning. Frail and tanned with strong cheekbones and wavy chestnut brown hair. Mash looked a lot like her. She cried at the sight of him standing in her doorway, speaking her language with what I assumed ended with many emphases after each word. "Vita! Vita!" she shouted.

Thumping noises came from the top of the house. A cute middle-aged woman peeped around the wall and shouted more words in Italian. I stood patiently by the door, watching the two women pinch Mash's cheeks and chin and hug him. It was the first time I saw him cry. Which led to me shedding a few tears.

Shortly, they settled down and he reached for my hand. I joined him at his side as he introduced me as his wife. Valeria held her face then held mine. "Bambino," she said.

My eyes widened and I responded, "No bambino, no bambino." I shook my head side to side.

'Hell no I'm not ready for that. Should I be offended?'

Vita then stood next to her and eyed me from head to toe. My heart pounded literally being in Valeria's hands. The two spoke Italian to each other briefly, and I looked over to Mash for help.

He placed his arm around me and joined their conversation, then Valeria sweetly said, "*Figlia*." She and Vita hugged me, gave me an extra once over, then pulled me by my arms to the sofa. I didn't understand a word the three of them were saying, but I picked up on *telefono* when Vita started making phone calls.

Within the hour, the house was packed with cousins and uncles from all over Vomero. The news Maximus was home travelled quickly, and the news he married a cocoa colored American surprisingly went better than I expected. His family showed me love and made me feel welcome, speaking in very little English and forcing me to eat. Our union received the warmest reception as his family blasted music and cooked food way into the night.

The former Mrs. Sharper wouldn't allow us to stay in the hotel we reserved. She forced us to stay with her in Mash's old room, with the thin walls, full size bed and loose headboard. We laughed most of the night, trying to sneak in a quick one, eventually giving up and dozing off.

By morning the house was already filled with family. Some who spent the night because it was a special occasion, and others who wanted to get a jump on the festivities. It was a repeat of the previous day. Family all around. Music blasting. People dancing. Matriarchs cooking. Children running. Everyone singing.

Before the sun set in the evening, my new cousins drove us around the never-ending hills to a spot overlooking the city, and Mount Vesuvius in the distance. The buildings looked like they were stacked on top of one another, but the sight was one to behold.

Cousin Primo convinced us to check out a sports bar where he bragged to any and every one, his cousin was famous. I put on a brave face as I watched everyone, except me go berserk when a team scored a point in the soccer match on the television. The place rocked with stomping and cheering, celebrations and beer splashing, from the tall glasses being thrown around.

The family kept the same energy when we returned to the house with more food, music still blasting, and more blankets laid out for the night. Seeing Mash around his family was an image I would always remember. He came from beautiful, loving people who instilled their values in him somehow from a distance. It was a side of him I needed to see, to cancel any doubt he was the one for me.

In the middle of the night he woke me, nibbling on my face. "You picked the best place for our honeymoon. What made you decide to come here?"

"Ibiza would have been ideal, but I know we're going back there this summer. And I wanted to meet your mom. Plus, I didn't want to go anywhere tropical."

"Why not?"

"Because I've been too embarrassed to tell you, I fall into the stereotype when it comes to water," I mumbled beneath my pillow.

"We do have a coast and seas you know."

"I know, but you don't think of boats, and oceans when you think of Pompeii. You think of the volcano and landmarks."

"True, but what stereotype?"

"I can't swim. I've tried to learn, but I can't hold my breath long under water, and when I try to move in the water, I go nowhere. It's quite comical."

"I can teach you."

"I will frustrate you."

"No, you won't. It'll be the first thing I teach you. The second will be how to make a proper mix."

"My mixes are fine."

"Remember I've seen your playlists." He joked and tapped my nose.

I squeezed his in return. We wrestled and giggled then he pressured me into taking a lesson from him. "I'll give it one lesson. But I'm telling you I'm pretty bad." I warned him.

"I love a challenge. I'll have you swimming like a fish by the end of the summer."

"God, you're confident. Go back to sleep."

"I had something else on my mind." He placed my hand on his wood.

"The walls are too thin," I whispered. "You know someone will hear us."

I rubbed his cock regardless of my excuse, breaking him free from his boxers. He tasted my lips. "I don't care. I want you now."

"I hate saying no to you." I sighed.

"Then don't."

I slipped under the covers and kissed him softly on the tip of his head, then slicked him with strong pulls from my throat to my lips. My plan was to suck him off quietly, so the family wouldn't hear the headboard knock against the wall, or squeaks from the bed as I was being pillaged. But my performance was stellar, and Mash's delight was far from quiet.

I rose from below and looked at him with a smile and shrugged my shoulders, then placed my finger over his lips. He flipped me over to the edge of the bed, then pulled me to my feet. I dropped to my knees for a second taste of him, gliding my hands against his abs, and looking him directly in his eyes. The taste of salt tinged my tongue. I froze and grinned at him.

He lifted me from the floor and bent me over facing the wall, boisterous in his delight, unconcerned with the listening ears. I restrained vocally, whimpering as low as possible, until the painful pleasure overpowered me. A gleeful sigh escaped when our skin slapped in rhythm as my husband placed one hand around my neck, bringing me closer to his body with a light choke to hold me in place. He grunted uncontrollably into my back, surely waking the house.

The next morning, I went into the kitchen, greeted with snickers from the aunts and my mother-in-law. It was obvious they heard us.

"What a beautiful glow you have this morning," said one of them in English, and the rest chuckled at my expense.

"It must be the water here," I replied.

"Mm hmm," said Valeria.

Italian words circled the room with giggles between them, *bambino* and *presto* frequently in their exchange. I smiled to let them know, I knew they were going in on me, then Mash and I left for a day out to ourselves.

Traffic was heavy on the short drive to Pompeii, but the scenic route made it worthwhile during the stall. The buildings along the route were picturesque, and the mosaics the first I had ever seen.

The closer we were to the city, we withdrew from our original plans of visiting the ruins, and roamed the streets instead. The highlight of the day was finally tasting what I heard was the best pizza in the world. I wasn't lied to. It was *magnifico*. I moaned with every bite, and didn't speak until I met the owner. After explaining how far I travelled to taste his heavenly pie, and commending him on its supreme flavor, he whispered his secret in my ear. *L'acqua naturale.*

Before returning to a house full of family, we strolled down the cobblestoned streets in the neighborhood, enjoying the starry night sky, searching for zodiac signs and visible planets. We picked up cartons of gelato for the little ones, and spent our final night with family trading stories— Mash translating for me, and eating until our bellies nearly burst.

The night ended with a surprise from Valeria. In front of the entire family, she placed a ring in Mash's hand. He translated her wish was for him to place her mother's ring on my finger, and made me promise to continue the tradition. I repeated, "*Lo prometto*," and the family cheered as Mash slid it in place.

The house remained filled with Pasini's for a final night, but it didn't stop us from repeating last night's activities— most likely being cheered on from every room in the house.

The next morning, we returned to business as usual, departing for Copenhagen. A one night stop, for a show I was not looking forward to attending. The name Harv Legend spilled from his lips as the headliner, and I laid low the moment we checked into the hotel.

Travel had gotten the best of me, so lounging in the room while Mash went to work wasn't a bad idea. Missing out on the famous crepe station, museums, and favorite spots Mash raved about, had to wait for a future visit. I was spent, leaving my bag packed due to our early departure merely hours away.

Mash arrived some time over in the night, lying next to me fully clothed. The alarm sounded and the in and out trip ended just as it began. The fact I didn't hear him when he arrived was telling of my exhaustion level.

To perk us up for the trip home, he stood in line at the bistro, fetching us coffee and scones, while I settled the bill at the desk. I reached for the receipt from the clerk and a hand snatched it away from my grasp.

"So, we meet again. I thought you were long gone back to America." Harv Legend grinned on the side of his mouth, continuing to be persistently annoying.

"Hello again. I hear you had an amazing show last night. Congrats. Now if you'll excuse me." I turned back to the clerk.

"How do you know we had a good show?"

"My husband told me."

"Husband? You and Mash?"

"Yes. Now if you'll excuse me."

"Queens belong with Kings." He grabbed my hand.

"Don't do that." I jerked away.

Folding the receipt in half, he toyed with me. Presenting and taking it away. I huffed in frustration, then he finally handed it to me. "Mash is cool, but he doesn't know what to do with a Queen like you."

I reached for the paper, and he held it tightly in his grip before letting it go. "And here I thought I got lucky running into you. Remember what I said." He rubbed my shoulder.

I maneuvered backwards, not knowing what to say or do as Mash appeared behind him. He reached forward and slapped his hand from my shoulder. "Harv, I thought we already went through this."

Harv's eyes grew big from the shock of Mash's actions. Stunned, he stared at Mash with a dumb look on his face, then attempted to deflect his wrongdoing. "I hear congratulations are in order. Seems like you would have mentioned that last night. But then again." He scoffed. "You two be easy."

'What does that mean?'

"Don't disrespect my wife again."

"Calm down big *mon. You no wan it wit a real bad mon,*" Harv jargoned.

"Let's just go," I said.

"Grimey fuck!" Mash groaned, and stood in front of me, protecting me by using his arm as a barrier.

"Oh you're a tough guy now?"

"I think you want to see if I'm a tough guy." Mash balled his fists.

"People are staring at us. Let's go. Please," I pled, pulling him away.

The matter wasn't discussed right away. Through checkpoint, the skywalk, and boarding, we avoided conversing with one another. I couldn't find the right words to say, and he wasn't in the right headspace to hear me. We were miles in the air before our eyes locked, and the silence was broken.

"Thank you for standing up for me." I leaned into him.

"I did what I was supposed to do." He kissed my forehead.

"I'm sorry that happened. I tried to handle it."

"Don't apologize for him. He was being a total wanker."

"You know you said were jealous, but you also have a bit of a temper. Promise me, you won't get into any trouble." I held onto his forearm.

"Don't worry. Everything will be fine."

But I was worried. Not because I was naïve, or believed life was a fairytale, though mine had been lately. I was worried if I had gotten out of my way, and gotten into his.

Upon exiting the airport, a massive number of alerts buzzed his phone. His demeanor worsened minute by minute, so I kept quiet as he fumed. We sat in the lot for at least half an hour as he rigorously texted, and stared off into space. '*How could I not be worried?*'

Eventually, he cranked the car and sat with a grimaced face. I was afraid to ask if everything was indeed fine. I sat quietly and uncomfortable on the ride home, waiting for him to offer some sort of an explanation. He didn't.

As the day grew sour by the hour, rest and relaxation

seemed ideal once we made it home. Thanks to the constant turn of events, it was hard to wind down, and I found myself doing what I always did whenever anxiety found its way into my space— I cooked like a madman and cleaned like a janitorial service.

I turned the rotting bananas into a banana nut loaf, and opened cans of tomatoes and added herbs and spices until the delightful smell of chili filled the house.

I unpacked, did a few loads of laundry, food prepped for the week, shampooed my hair and dusted around the house with the conditioner dripping, and changed the linens.

Mash had been on his phone since we returned, blowing on smoke out by the pool. He suddenly called for me. "Put on your bathing suit!"

I ignored him.

Moments later he shouted, "Let's go!" His calls went unanswered. He came inside and cornered me with red eyes, and a goofy smirk— high as a kite, feeling good no doubt. "Outside now."

He wouldn't take no for an answer, so I gave him my word I would be out in five minutes. I dressed in my suit, and grabbed towels for the both of us. Standing near the sliding door, I overheard him on a call with a gentleman constantly repeating, "We've got to fix this. We've got to fix this!"

"She's my wife. Cancel all future shows with him." I heard him say.

My worst fear had come true. My being in his life was creating chaos. I gripped the door handle, frozen in time, listening to the conversation while my mind got the best of me.

"I'm sure if he knew she was your wife he would have never disrespected you," said the male voice from the speaker.

"He was out of line. On the contrary, he knew she was with me."

"And what are you doing getting married? It goes against the image we've worked so hard to give you."

"What are you saying?"

"Your brand is at risk if word gets out you have a wife. Girls see you as the hot deejay they want to spend a night with, and the shows sell based on that fantasy. Women are 70% of your audience and fan base."

"Wow, Davie. And here I was thinking it was my mixes and musical talent drawing in the crowds."

"You and I both know this business is about more than talent. And you are talented kid, but this is the world we live in. You've got to work with me here. Do me a favor and keep the news of your nuptials quiet for now. I'll be in touch in a few days with word on how we are going to spin this."

The door jolted and I was busted standing there. There was no need to pretend I wasn't eavesdropping, so I confessed, "I heard every word. I'm sorry you're going through all of this because of me. I haven't told anyone we eloped yet, so the secret is safe with me."

The goofy look had disappeared from his face. It was now blank, and I didn't know how to read him.

"You're not a secret," he said.

'That's good to know.'

"Let's do this another day. I'm not in the mood to learn tonight."

"No. We're doing it now."

"Has anyone ever told you, you were bossy?" I playfully asked.

He lifted me in his arms and threw me in the shallow side. I stood up in the water and he jumped in beside me, "You're the first to tell me that. Now do as I say." I looked at him like he was crazy and we laughed. "In all seriousness, show me what you can do," he said in a sweeter tone.

Embarrassing myself, I went under and did the moves as I always had, then returned to the surface. It was laughable, but he didn't make fun of me. Instead he put his arms around me and said, "You're going to do just fine. Lesson one, go under again and open your eyes this time."

"No. It stings. I need goggles."

"Get comfortable not having them.. Take your time. We've got all night."

I went under countless times, but never opened my eyes. I waited for him to grow impatient with me, but he didn't, which I found frustrating. Again and again I buried my head, insisting we give up, but he wouldn't allow it.

My frustration soon turned into anger, then finally I did it. We stared at each other for a brief moment beneath the surface, then he smiled at me. I rose to the top, wiped my eyes and pushed my hair back. My patient instructor swam to me and gave me a kiss, proud of my effort, not giving a damn about the chaos going on outside of our house.

The following afternoon we were back at it. I was told to get comfortable with my opening my eyes in the water, before learning how to properly hold my breath below. Up and down he moved my head with a three count, relentless with his method. *'God he will not let up.'*

One hour— every day— I had a lesson. Kicks, strokes, and breathing techniques. By the end of the week I was floating on my back and swimming a small distance. It was a small victory for him, but a huge one for myself.

I was instructed to stay out of the pool, while he fulfilled his contractual obligations over the weekend with Harv Legend. The ink was barely dry of making our marriage legal, and we were already in the midst of our first hurdle— because of me.

His career and brand was facing ruin, he was now at odds

with a longtime colleague, disputing with his management, and having to lie about his personal life. I couldn't help but feel responsible. My compromise to abandon my home seemed trivial, compared to what he was facing, and I was the common denominator of these newfound problems.

To ease my sorrows, I opened a bottle of wine to keep me company for the evening, ending in a drunken stupor. Mash called after sound check, sharing the details of his meeting with his PR team and Davie, his manager, "I'm not on board with the way they want to spin. They want me to deny I'm married in interviews, and stage photos eluding I'm dating around." He seethed.

He sounded terribly flustered, and I wasn't in the right frame of mind to pacify his frustration. Primarily because I blamed myself.

"I was thinking, maybe I should leave. Not because I want to, but because it's the right thing to do. Let's face it, you wouldn't be in this mess if it weren't for me."

"Rubbish. How much have you had?" He laughed.

"I'm almost done with this bottle, but I'm speaking facts. Your life can go back to normal if I wasn't here." I rambled.

"I told you not to worry. I'm taking care of it." He exhaled deeply. "You should have been here with me. I'd be all over you right now. Show me something to hold me over."

I flashed my breast and screamed of embarrassment. Mash blushed and grinned, promising he'd be home as soon as the final show closed, while I promised to sleep off the tipsiness.

It pained me to be the root cause of his drama. My feelings were being spared, but the truth was the truth. The last thing I wanted was to be his downfall, and when the alcohol wore off in the morning, I opened my notebook and wrote a pro and con list of our relationship.

I was halfway down the page when I received a notification

on my phone. I took a pause and learned I had a new follower on social media, a few direct messages, and one missed call from Khai. I sent her a message that I would call her later, then checked my social account.

"Son of a bitch!" I shouted. My new follower turned out to be Harv Legend, and the direct messages were from him, along with a photo of a woman and Mash in what perceived to be a deep conversation.

My chest felt as though it could cave in. My head felt a sharp pain from the back that pierced like a yo-yo, and I threw my phone to the opposite side of the bed.

Wanting to look at the pictures again, but knowing I shouldn't. I jumped up and painted the floor with my slippers, dragging my feet while coming up with an explanation of what I saw to soothe my soul. I looked out of the window, then caught a glimpse of myself in the glass. It was as if outside mimicked how I felt inside, as the rain depicted tears on my face before they fell. *'This can't be happening.'*

The first tear fell and I dialed Mash. No answer. I tried a second time. No answer. I needed to hear him say nothing happened last night, or the picture was taken before we met, or the photo was staged, and he had no choice but to go along with his manager's ridiculous plan this one time. Anything. I needed to hear his voice give me a reasonable explanation to make my rage go away.

After he didn't answer the third time, a million worse case scenarios plagued my thoughts. I went back to the photograph and examined it. The malicious Harv Legend uprooted my world with this image. I enlarged it looking for the wedding band, the hotel name in the background, or a logo of some sort. Finally, I caved and read the message attached:

From what I saw tonight you are fair game.

I told you Queens belong with Kings
@ me.

Immediately I thought of what he said that morning he and Mash squared up. "Seems like you would have mentioned that last night. But then again..."

'What did he mean then, and what did he mean now?'

The longer I didn't hear from Mash, the more enraged I became. My thoughts got the best of me as I waited for my phone to ring. Harv ran a brilliant number on me. Since I had time to think, I realized I was caught in a trap.

If I mentioned the photo to Mash and who sent it to me, he would most likely lose his temper, and only God knows what would happen— but I would be at fault for telling him. If I waited to show him the messages when he got home, I would be blamed for not telling him right away. It was the typical conundrum for a woman— always holding the blame no matter what.

Within seconds, I skipped being mad, jumped over angry, bypassed rage, and embraced crazy. The drama, questionable deceit, and humiliation was too much for me to handle, on top of already feeling like the catalyst of a potential downfall. And the fact that I failed to reach my husband after three attempts. Multiple scenarios ran through my mind:

'Is he with her right now?
Is that why he didn't answer my call?
Why the fuck would he play me like this?
Is this a staged photo his PR put together?
How can a person make you feel so loved,
and betray you at the same time?
It doesn't make sense.
What are my friends going to think?
God I look stupid. Again! I know he loves me.
He treats me like any woman
would dream of being treated.
Will I ever know the truth? I trusted him.
What the fuck is going on!'

Then it hit me. I had seen the girl in the photo before. I ran to the bedroom and flipped through his albums until I searched the right one. It was the memory book with the pretty models and famous people. There she was. Smiling in at least ten or more pictures with him.

I threw the album across the room, breathing heavily like a monster. Unable to calm down, I went into the kitchen and threw myself into some serious cooking and baking. My go to when I'm stressed.

I baked and prepared casserole dishes, two flavors of cookie dough, eating the chocolate chip dough raw. I baked a sourdough loaf and sautéed peppers and onions to dress up a sandwich. I stood against the island and took a bite, bursting into tears, spitting the perfectly dressed hoagie on the floor to catch my breath.

I wasn't this woman. I didn't want to be this woman. I didn't like this woman, as I had already been her years before. The fairytale was over, and I was tired and defeated. I dumped on myself for abandoning my okay life, for what I thought was a better one, and could no longer fight the inevitable.

I packed what I could in two suitcases, and framed a picture of us in Italy, I had stuck in the crevice of the mirror on the dresser. I placed it in the center of the pool table in the dining room, and said good-bye to the house I thought was going to be my home. The taxi called for entry through the gate, and I lugged my bags outside and set the alarm. As the driver drove me away, a song I used to know so well came on the radio, and I sang along to it in my head. *'Good morning heartache, what's new.'*

CHAPTER 10
REALISM

The credit from my cancelled flight months ago came in handy. I caught the next flight into the States, Denver, then waited two hours for a layover to GSP. I silenced my phone for a "peace" of mind and roamed the airport, searching for the apocalyptic art people raved about. Creepy as fuck. Fires, coffins, and weird looking children of the corn figures.

I love art but the one mural I found was made of nightmares. I went back to my gate, beyond happy to get the hell out of Satan's airport.

The real home of home. Mama's house. My voice of reason. I don't think she's ever hugged me so tight, or so long. To be in her embrace soothed my bleeding soul, and just like that I felt like a little girl again. Her house wasn't the house I grew up in, but the scent of it was the same. A blend of roasted coffee and baked goods lived inside the walls, with a hint of bleach and ammonia in the air.

We sat in the kitchen playing catch up, waiting for the

timer to ding, to take her sweet bread out of the oven. I turned my phone on to show her pictures of my travels with continuous interruptions of texts, calls, and voice messages.

"Something seems important. You ought to get that," she said.

"It can wait. I wanted to show you one picture in particular."

"Oh my. Weren't you a smashing bride." Ma held her chest. "When was this?"

"About a month ago."

"When do I get to meet my new son? Is this what you came home to tell me?"

"Sort of?" I fidgeted.

"Well you don't need my approval because it's already done. And you know I was going to tell you, you looked beautiful as ever. So, what is it?"

"I think it's over."

My mother laughed deep from her belly. The timer dinged and she removed the bread from the oven and placed it on top of a towel, on top of the toaster. Sighing and making comical noises she asked, "Over. Why?"

"It's a long story."

"It always is." She scoffed.

"And before you say it, I know marriage takes work but... We've hit a huge bump in the road."

"Is it that bad? Because honey to be honest, you look happy to me."

"I was happy, but I don't think I'm going back."

"What do you mean was? I know the look of love when I see it. Especially on my baby."

The phone rang again. "Is that him?" Ma asked.

I nodded yes, unable to survive her stare.

"Talk to him," she said.

"I need more time."

"Okay Ms. Need More Time. Some other woman is going to take your time."

"One already has. I think."

"Start from the beginning."

Mom listened to my dilemma, and shared a story with me about perspective and perception. She went on to tell me that sometimes things aren't what they seem, and without me hearing what Mash had to say, I was making a mistake. "A picture is worth a thousand words," she said. "People don't always have good intentions. Are you going to allow the person who sent you that photo, to control your happiness?"

After making her point, she finished schooling me by saying as long as I knew the truth about the fake pictures, other people's insight shouldn't matter. "People are going to think whatever they want to think anyway, and in a marriage, communication can make it or break it," she said, handing me a slice of the warm bread.

I sat on the stool nearly healed from the taste of my mother's cooking, ready to hear my husband's explanation. I returned his call and he answered on the first ring, looking at me through the glass with seething eyes in utter silence. "Hey," I mumbled.

He took a few seconds to respond. "What the fuck babe, I've been calling you all day."

I was shocked by his callous tone and word choice. "I turned off my ringer. I needed to figure some things out."

We sat in silence, waiting for the other to speak. "Why did you leave?" he asked, in a softer tone than before. "Where are you and when are you coming home?"

"At my mother's house, and I don't know the answer to that question."

"You have no idea how I'm feeling right now. I rushed home to be with you, and find you've left me. And for what?"

"For starters, I don't want you to resent me. I don't want to be the reason you lose everything you've worked for."

"I would never resent you. I told you to let me worry about work. Come home."

My heart rate increased and my palms began to sweat. There wasn't an easy way to ask him about the picture. I blurted out, "Did anything happen this weekend? Something I should hear from you and no one else."

"I have no idea what you're talking about."

"Check your phone. I sent you something."

We stared at each other through our screens, waiting for the message to transmit. "Bloody hell. Where did you get this?" he asked.

"Harv sent it to me."

"Bollocks! That barmy maggot! Is this why you left?"

"Who is she?" I demanded.

"No one. Nadia, I don't know what else to do to show you I love you."

"I know you love me."

"Then why are you giving up on us so easily? I promise you. It's nothing. I will explain everything to you. But I want to do it in person. I need you to know I would never do anything to hurt you."

Having to wait for him to explain the image infuriated me. I didn't need an answer in person. I just needed clarity. My hesitation to answer his question bothered him, so he asked it again.

"You know I would never hurt you, right?"

I huffed and scowled at him. "That's what makes this so hard. I believe you. It's a lot to take in, but I believe you. What confuses me is the picture, and the things Harv says. In Copenhagen, he made that remark about you, and now he's saying from what he saw I'm now fair game? All of this code language makes me wonder what is he not saying."

"He's being a dick. I'll take care of him. You, take some time. You did say you were homesick, so do whatever it is you need to do, and I'll tell you everything when you get back. You still love me?"

"I wouldn't be hurt if I didn't love you."

The pain in my chest didn't leave after we spoke. It felt like a wrecking ball knocked the wind out of me, and left a huge dent in between my breasts. I was more confused than when I left, and tossed all night with a cloudy mind. I beat the sun and my mother up, and suggested we drive to Goose Creek to pay my Grams a visit.

Mom skimmed through my phone, admiring the photos of my travels while I sped down the highway, arriving at the retirement village in record time.

After two and a half hours of listening to the oldies at the crack of dawn, we signed our names in the record book, and I powerwalked to my grandmother's room. Seeing her never failed to brighten my day, and I was long overdue for one of her hugs.

I peeped my head into her room. She sat in her rocking chair, dressed comfortably in a blush sweat suit with her long, silver silky hair pulled behind her ears, and braided to the side. I was jealous my hair never grew as long as hers, but I did inherit her texture and wave pattern, which made up for what I lacked. "There is my pretty lady?" I said, entering her room.

She turned to her side and looked at me, fanning her hand and turning up her top lip. "Well, gal why didn't you tell me you were coming? It's been a long time." She kissed my cheeks. "You still got a little sugar in there."

"You know I love surprising you," I said, kissing her forehead.

I held onto her tightly, smelling her perfume from the 1950's mixed with mink oil, and dove soap. She patted me on the shoulder. "Yes, you sure do. You look good gal. Skin so plump and smooth."

"I am the chocolate version of you."

"Which is even better. Less wrinkles when you get old."

Ma finally arrived in the room. "Leave some hugs for me." Grams turned towards her and gave mom her cheek.

"Oh, I got both of you today. Is the good-looking boy with you, too?"

"Momma behave."

"You know I will do no such thing."

I told her I came alone and she asked to see another picture of Mash. I pulled up some of our travel photos, and showed her how to swipe left and right. "This sure is from the future." She scoffed, then arrived to the one of us in Barcelona. "Nadia, you are every bit of me I tell you what. I would've married him too if it was safe back in my day. My baby girl snagged her a husband. Such a handsome boy. Grams can dig it."

"Momma." My mother ridiculed.

"What *chile*? You are always cramping my style. You know that's why I won't come live with her. I'd never get to see my boyfriends if I moved in her jailhouse."

"Did you say boyfriends with an s?" I asked.

"You heard me right. I have one on every hall in here."

"How is that possible?" my mother asked.

"Easy. One is a night hawk, one is in a wheelchair, and the other one can't half see."

"I've missed you so so much Grams?" I curled over in laughter.

"If they have men my age over there who look like him, I'll move in with you baby girl. Book my ticket tonight."

"Momma please. You aren't moving anywhere."

"You hear the sheriff talkin' right?" Grams joked.

"Okay I'm ringing the bell. You two always go at it. How have you been doing?"

"Really good today, but I have my days, arthritis and all."

"You feel like getting out of here today?" I asked.

"Hell yeah, if you're not too tired. I want to see the water. I can smell it for God's sake, so I'd like to see it."

"Let's go."

On our way to the beach, I noticed The Creek had been updated since my last visit. I remembered it as nine busy streets surrounded by green landscape and moss trees. Now mom and pop businesses and shopping plazas stood in lots that were once flat grassed terrain. The amount of street lights doubled if not tripled, and the population and diversity was significantly diverse.

In less than an hour, Grams removed her shoes and walked bare feet in the sand until she reached the water. She looked like a young woman as she played footsie with the waves and dusting off seashells. I could tell from her smile she was reminiscing of old times, and mom and I watched her become one with the sand as the grains sifted between her toes.

I joined her in the water, while Mom stood in line at the booth for chair rentals. Grams and I were in sync, and she hurried in one of our special talks for the few moments we had alone.

"My gal went and got married on me," she said.

"Are you mad finding out this way?"

"Not at all. All I care about is you being happy. Are you happy?"

"That's a complicated answer Grams. I love him."

"Hell, I would love him, too. But happiness is what I want for you."

"I'm happy, we just have a few wrinkles that need ironing."

"I'm sure you'll tell me all about it when you're ready. Just remember. You ain't nobody's fool. If you can't get the wrinkles out, get a new shirt. Uh oh, here comes the warden."

Listening to the waves roar a few feet away, we stretched beneath three rented beach chairs and umbrellas. Basking in the breeze with worthy conversation between three generations for hours, I forgot about my dilemma for a short while. My mind needed that break, and my soul needed what my grandmother had always given me— strength.

Once the sun set, we grabbed a quick bite to eat, and said good-bye to Grams. We headed back upstate where I spent a few more days with my mother, then I returned to Charlotte, to the abandoned place I called my own.

Khai had done a great job taking care of my plants. I did a thorough walkthrough, dusting what needed to be dusted, changed the linens to fresh washed sheets, tossed the spoiled milk from the fridge, sorted my mail, and settled in. I pulled out my laptop and stared at a blank page, not knowing where to begin, and realizing I had nothing to come back to.

Before the five o'clock traffic began, I surprised Khai at work. Popping my head in her office I teased. "They said the weed man is in here."

"Oh my God! What are you doing here?! Is this why you didn't call me back?!" She hugged me.

'Oops I forgot to return her missed call the day the chaos erupted.'

"This trip was a spur of the moment thing," I said.

"Is Mash with you?"

"No, he had to work." I sort of lied.

"So we can get some girl time in?"

"Yes. I'm in desperate need."

We met the girls at one of the better, and upscale clubs in the city for happy hour. While we waited, Khai ordered appetizers and the first round of drinks, filling me in on what her phone call was about.

Taylor and Levi were having marital problems, but no one knew the reason why, and her father-in-law moved in with her family, so she's been using my house as an escape. Before she finished telling me about the strain it has put on her marriage, Shannon arrived.

"What's up Grandma Klump? You remembered us little people!"

I stood to hug her as Isla waved her hand and spoke in a fake British accent, "Lady Nadia has decided to grace us with her presence. To what do we owe the pleasure?"

"It's good to see you too, Isla." I scowled.

We air kissed cheek to cheek as Taylor surprised me from behind. "You finally came home," she said, squeezing my shoulders.

"It took me a minute, but I finally made it. Now give me all the tea."

Shannon lit up like a light bulb, describing her latest boy toy while Isla kept the details of her mystery man secret.

"How are you and Levi doing?" I asked Taylor.

She moaned something jumbly under her breath and deflected. "How is London?"

"I don't know. It was great at first, but now...I have a lot of decisions to make."

"Would these decisions have to do with you getting married and not telling us." Taylor snitched.

"How did you know?"

"We all know. Mash told Levi, and Levi swore me to secrecy, but you know I had to tell the girls."

"I wanted to tell y'all in person, and show you the ring his mother passed down to me. You want to see pictures?"

They passed my phone around and swiped while I gave them the details of Barcelona and how Mash proposed, how beautiful Italy was, and how I made my head wrap for our ceremony.

"Look at you with those flowers in your hair. Levi and I should have done this. Simple, intimate and romantic," said Taylor.

"Your wedding was beautiful Tay." Everyone at the table synchronized to pacify her.

"Humph." She scoffed.

Khai gave me the side eye. She spoke of marital problems between Taylor and Levi, and it was clear something was going on there.

Taking the negative light off of Taylor, I mentioned Mash's management wants us to keep the marriage a secret— curious to see how they would respond, and who would agree with me.

"I say go along with the lie," said Taylor. "His image is his livelihood, and from what I saw, it's worth it to lie."

"Sorry, but I would want everyone to know I'm the wife," said Isla.

"What does Mash have to say about all of this?" Khai asked.

"He says I'm not a secret and not to worry. But I feel like I'm in his way."

"Did he say that?" Shannon frowned at me.

"No."

"Then stop doing the Nadia thing and jumping to conclusions." Shannon offered.

"The Nadia thing?"

"You know what you do," they said in unison.

I clutched my fake pearls at their synchronized depiction of me. Once again, I was the butt of the joke, but it was fine. We laughed as if nothing had changed over the months I was away, but something had. Me.

I couldn't bring myself to show them the picture, or tell them the full story of my dealings across the ocean. The old me would have blabbed every detail, but the new me chose to be happy in the moment, and to keep some things to herself.

CHAPTER 11
ARRIVEDERCI

N ow what? I was no longer homesick. Mom was doing fine without me, my friends were carrying on, and our reunion was just like old times.

A night of embarrassing photos and laughs, relieved me from my racing thoughts. But now it was morning, and with it came a hangover from hell, loneliness, and the constant question burdening my brain. *'What should I do?'*

I was lying on my favorite high thread count sheets with one eye open, and the other closed like Uncle Fester, when the doorbell rang. I robed and opened the door, greeted to orchids at my feet. I shouted to the delivery man, "Wait! I'll get you a tip!"

He replied, "No need! It's already been taken care of! Thanks!"

The card read:

Counting the days ~ Love Mash

I grabbed a juice and a stale bagel from the fridge, toasted it, took a bite, and threw it in the garbage. Above the trash can was my calendar with a red circle on today's date, which meant there was a group meeting tonight. I searched for something else to snack on, but only found crackers, took them with me upstairs, and texted Mash.

N: *I love you, too.*

I reacquainted myself with my sheets, and slept until hunger woke me a few hours later. I dressed for what remained of the day, then drove to my favorite mom and pop pizza shop across town to give my taste buds a pinch of heaven.

Bell and banana peppers, onions, and cheese on a soft doughy crust— just as I remembered. I closed my eyes as the taste soothed my soul, when suddenly, I thought of Italy. I couldn't help but compare it to the best pizza I ever had, forcing me to smile at the good times.

Bored and avoiding my lonely house, I drove to the building where Dr. Bartley held her sessions, then kept on driving arriving at Taylor's house. The tension was thick between she and Levi, a knife wouldn't suffice. She begged me to stay longer than I intended, and when I finally broke free I thought of a saying Grams used to teach me. *'If God took all the problems and threw them in the air, everyone would grab their own.'*

She was absolutely right. Feeling their vibe propelled me to reach out to London. I was ready to hear his explanation and make a decision. But just like the day I left, no answer.

The next morning, I shopped for grocery and prepared my homemade salsa and guac for bowling night. Another night out with my friends, was better than sitting alone in the house thinking about my problems, and why I hadn't heard from my husband.

The crowd at the alley was mixed with newcomers and old faces. Some I recognized from the wedding, and others I couldn't place. The groomsman I danced with at the reception served as a buffer and made a joke at my expense.

"Hey Mrs. Copperfield," he said. "One minute I saw you in London, then the next minute you vanished."

"Sounds like me. Drew, right? Levi's college buddy?"

"Yeah. I asked about you a few times, but Levi said I moved too slow. He said you stayed over there and got married?"

"I did."

"Was it the guy you were dancing with?"

"You saw us?"

"Everyone did."

I smiled, remembering Khai said the exact same thing to me.

"Time to whoop ass!" Brian, Khai's husband yelled.

"Congratulations, and good luck tonight." Drew winked his eye at me as he walked off.

"Your team is the one who needs it." I snapped my fingers.

We separated into teams and began the competition, Mars versus Venus. Alcohol always led to a night of laughs and an occasional altercation. Towards the end of the first round, the women were leading on the scoreboard, and the men were losing gracefully.

It was a drama free night, and after we took round one we huddled for some girl talk, while the losers stormed the bar to buy the second-round drinks.

"Someone told me when you get married, you become more desirable. Is that true Nadia?" Shannon asked.

"I would say yes."

"Me, too," Khai added. "I've had men come out of the woodworks, but the gag is those men wouldn't marry a soul. They just want to fuck you and send you back home."

"Khai you cursed!" We gasped.

"Well it's true."

"Women are no different. They want to sleep with your man just so they can stare you down and throw it in your face," Shannon added.

"You would know." Isla teased.

Shannon invaded Isla's personal space and danced in a raunchy manner. The two playfully tussled, entertaining us until Taylor interrupted. "Why are we talking about this?"

We looked to one another, realizing we were close to getting answers of what was going on in her house. Khai changed the subject. "I heard Isla went hummus shopping."

Isla hid her face and blushed, then looked at me. "I don't know how you do it. We had nothing in common."

"You have to get the right one." I bragged.

"By the way, our friends want us to fix whatever is going on between us. Are we good?" Isla tested me.

"We're good." I held out my hand to shake for a truce.

"Ladies, get your pretty asses up! We are about to redeem ourselves!" Levi announced.

Team Venus went toe to toe with Team Mars throwing strikes, turkeys, trash talking, and celebrating with in-your-face choreographed routines. The men drank so much beer, we thought we had an edge on them until the final frame, where we lost by a gutter ball from our weakest link.

The night was young and the party continued at Khai's house. Brian cranked up the grill, Khai brought games outside near the pool, and Shannon's new beau took charge of the music.

As I watched the couples interact, happily and miserably, I realized I was ready to go home, and not the one a few blocks over. The one on the cusp of daylight, with the man I wanted to be happy and miserable with. *'Guess I have made up my mind.'*

Stepping away from the party, I eased over by the fence for privacy and finally made contact with London. Something was off. I could hear it in his voice. He was vague and sounded on edge, which unnerved me. Our conversation was short, and it felt like I was talking to a stranger. Not one I love you at the end. I wondered if our time apart gave him clarity— I was indeed bringing him down, and with all of the awkward silence between us, I didn't mention I was ready to come home.

After my uninspiring phone call, I returned to the party to tell everyone I was going to call it a night. "Don't go," they all said, convincing me to stay a while longer.

Caving into their request, I hung around and pretended to be fine when I was losing it inside. I circled the yard one final time, making sure I spoke to everyone before I made my exit, then did the unthinkable. I removed my sandals and jumped in the pool.

"Somebody go in there and get her!"

"She doesn't know how to swim!"

I rose to the top.

"Yes I do!" I yelled.

Three seconds under, rise to the top. Three seconds under, rise to the top. I swam from one side to the other as my friends grew louder and louder, muffled under the water. I reached up for the edge and pulled myself to the surface.

Water dripped from my hair and into my eyes as I stood in the shallow, smiling from ear to ear clearing my face.

"So you're a show off now," the deep voice said.

I opened my eyes to a grinning Mash kneeling before me. "Hey you," I said, lifting myself higher to meet his lips as fast as I could. "What are you doing here?"

He pulled me out of the water. "I came to bring you home."

My soaked clothing dampened his as I pressed against him, locking my lips with his as if it were for the first time. Chatter in the background didn't break my concentration. I was in the arms of the one I wanted to be with, and didn't let go of his tongue until our hosts shouted, "Get a room!"

"Who knew he was coming here?" I asked.

"Just me," said Levi. "My wife can't keep a secret."

I gave him a fist motion.

"Levi, you said it was hot down here. You should have said boiling." Mash joked.

He removed his shirt and his shoes, picked me up, and I wrapped my legs around him. I hugged him tightly around his neck, and screamed as he leaped in the pool. My eyes closed when I felt the water on my feet, but I opened them once Mash pinched me, and kissed him underwater.

We rose from the deep end, my arms still around him, spinning and playing in the water, convincing the others to join us.

The night ended with a splash party, Mash and I abandoned before everyone else. I skipped the tour and led Mash to my bedroom. Our bedroom. I was in a rush to feel him inside me, but he took his time to give me what I wanted.

He shampooed my hair in the shower, building up the sensual stamina to come. I was in agony, yearning for our bodies to bond once more. He kissed me after every rinse, teasing me with finger play in between. I shuddered from the cold air blowing above, then warmed with heat when he tasted my quivering lips between my thighs.

I turned my back to him, but he had something else in mind. He lifted me between my legs and carried me to the bed. On my knees, I fell atop the satin spread, and he held me in place grazing my ass cheeks with his teeth.

He spread them apart and wet his fingers, massaging my

forbidden with gentle, circular strokes. Screams of passion parted my lips as my face was buried, muffling my cry, until he lied me on my back.

I squirmed even though I hungered for him. "You remember how to take it. Look at me," he said, and submitted his plow. I clutched on to him as tight as I could, moaning and sighing in his ear. "Good girl. Oh, how I've missed your sugar." He dug deeper and faster.

Abruptly he positioned me on my side to the edge of the bed, digging in me sideways, yowling at the touch of a newfound corner as I switched between circular motions, and galloping charges from my throbbing womb. I spread my ass open so he could see his excavation, heightening his intensity. Barely keeping quiet he held onto my shoulders, and released his load while locked inside of me.

My drip held her grip while I waited for him to regain his strength, and release me from his hold. I clutched and vibrated on his wood, happy to have him where he belonged. I thought about when he said wherever we are together is home, and he was right. I belonged at his side, and he was home for me.

Lying next to me, he ran his hands through my hair then all over my body, studying my face while adorning me. "How do you feel?"

I panted. "Like all is right with the world."

"It is now. I missed you. I baked the cookies you left in the fridge, and it made me think of how you only eat the crispy ends and give me the middle, then I was reminded of how you don't eat the crispy end of cake. I can't make sense of it." He mocked.

"I know I'm quirky."

"Yes, you are. But I fell in love with quirky."

"I'm already lying here naked, you don't have to flatter me."

"I also fell in love with that swift tongue of yours."

"It's not the only thing you fell in love with."

He rolled me on top of him, sweeping my face, and reading my eyes. I played with the stubble on his chest searching for words, unaware I was putting him to sleep. He was tired and so was I, but I stayed awake until he drifted off, then laid my head on his shoulder, giving in to the night taking us under its spell.

In the morning, he told me he signed with new management, and we could move on from the nonsense. I spoke my truth and told him I didn't want to be kept a secret, and we agreed to move one from that narrative.

I waited for him to bring up the weekend in Cardiff. It was clear he was avoiding the subject when he mentioned how great my bed felt. It did sleep well, but it wasn't top grade like our bed in London. It cost significantly less, wasn't nearly as soft, and I personally upgraded his sheet thread count when I moved in.

I lifted from his chest and took it upon myself to bring up the matter. "Just tell me nothing happened so I can calm my mind."

"Nadia, nothing happened. Harv knows I despise her. He saw it as a way to get back at me. Reaching at its finest."

"I don't want to ever feel like that again. I drove myself crazy with theories. I needed to hear you say this is nothing. But then you didn't answer your phone, and I lost it. Deep down I know you wouldn't do anything to hurt me, but looking at that picture over and over gave me a little doubt."

He kissed my hands and stroked my hair. "The night of that picture, I told her I would file a restraining order if she came to any more of my shows."

"Who is she?"

"An old friend."

"And she was in Copenhagen, am I right?"

"Yes. But can we not talk about her?"

Normally, I would have badgered him and made him tell me everything I wanted to know, but I trusted my gut and left it alone. "I was thinking, since we're both here we might as well file for a marriage license, so I can change my last name before we go back."

"I love that idea Mrs. Sharper."

THE PAPERS WERE FILED and Maximus Sharper was properly introduced to his mother-in-law. Determined to have me wed in a traditional setting, we stood in church with her after Sunday service, and said our vows at the hands of her pastor.

Mash surprised me with a written vow, using the pro and con list of our relationship I wrote the night I was in distress. He said to the congregation, "I won't read everything on this paper, because I've crossed out the things that don't matter. My wife needed several reassurances of my love for her, and being the analytical person she is, she compiled a list I found. I've walked around with it in my wallet for good luck ever since, and I want to let her know that her list is also my list. My wife Nadia— She makes me happy. I have grown as a person because of her, and having her in my life has changed me for the better. And I love her. I love her. I love her. She also wrote I taught her how to swim, but I would like to add, she taught me what happiness is."

My mother's pastor didn't get a chance to say the words – *You may now kiss your bride.* Mash reeled me in and kissed me before the words left his mouth, becoming man and wife in front of family and friends, making it official on two continents.

Fear no longer controlled me. I was no longer afraid of

change, and ready to live life abroad with a man who is incomparable, and worthy of me. Excitement filled me for our journey ahead, leaving my old life behind, and beginning a new chapter that felt promising in a foreign land. The place I now call home.

THE LIST

Cons: ~~Interference with career, drama with colleagues, jealousy, financially challenged.~~

Pros: Makes me happy, changed for the better, grown as a person, sleep better next to him, taught me to swim, I love him, I love him, I love him.

Thank you for diving into my fictional worlds. These characters reappear in a mashup novella with the cast featured from my On Track But Off Course Series, 'My Gift To You: Levi & Launa Find Love'.

 facebook.com/t.k.richards

 instagram.com/t.k.richards

 tiktok.com/@tkrwrites

 youtube.com/tkrichards

 pinterest.com/tkwrites

REVIEWS ENCOURAGE VORACIOUS INTEREST EVERY WHERE TO SUPPORT

ME, THE AUTHOR

I GREATLY APPRECIATE IT

XOXO

FIND OUT WHAT HAPPENS NEXT & CHECK OUT OTHER TOP SELLING ROMANCE BY T.K. RICHARDS

A Taste of the Forbidden

https://books2read.com/atasteoftheforbidden

A Taste of the Forbidden

The Vampiress

Juke: A Love Story

T.K. RICHARDS is a multi-genre author of women's fiction and romance, featuring popular novels and novellas in Black Romance, Interracial/Multicultural Romance, Paranormal Romance, and YA Fiction. You can find her serialized fiction work on the Kindle Vella app. A graduate of Limestone University, T.K. has honors in Expository Writing, and was also the Poet Laureate of her graduating class. When she is not writing, she is immersed in the world of tennis, and binge watching movies—mostly comedy as she loves to laugh.

For more information about **T.K. Richards**, visit her website at www.tkrichards.com or subscribe to her newsletter at: https://tkrichardsnewsletter.ck.page

You can follow T.K. RICHARDS on the platforms listed below to interact with her personally:

facebook.com/Tkrichards

x.com/tkrichards1

instagram.com/t.k.richards

pinterest.com/TKWrites

tiktok.com/@tkrwrites

youtube.com/tkrichards

goodreads.com/T.k.richards

bookbub.com/authors/t-k-richards

amazon.com/author/Tkrichards

BY T.K. RICHARDS

Made in the USA
Columbia, SC
01 March 2024